BREAKING

BENJAMIN

HAYLEE THORNE
MICHELLE WINDSOR

First published May 2018
Copyright © Haylee Thorne 2018
Copyright © Michelle Windsor 2018
Published by
Windsor House Publishing
Cover Design by Liv Moore at Liv's Shoppe
Copy editing provided by Kendra Gaither at Kendra's Editing and Book Services
Formatting provided by Formatting by Leigh

This one is for the fans of The Auction Series and The Kingsley Series....

Without you, there may not have been a Ben and Jill.

We hope you love them as much as we love you.

CHAPTER ONE

I shove two fingers between my collar and neck and tug hard as I stride through the revolving door of our newest hotel. This damn tie is strangling me. It's bad enough I have to make an appearance at these events, but Drew's insistence that I wear a suit and tie is pure torture for me and he knows it. Fuck it. I grasp the knot of the tie, loosen it, and yank the noose-like silk over my head, shoving the offending article in my jacket pocket. I unbutton the top two buttons of my shirt as well, letting out a sigh of pleasure at the ability to breathe freely again. What's Drew going to do, fire me? He can't. I own thirty percent of the company, just like him.

Just to really get under his skin, I stop at the coat check, swap my suit jacket for a ticket, and grin widely. I thank the attendant who has just unwittingly helped me to drag at least one eye roll out of my younger brother this evening. Yep, Drew is my younger brother, but he does more to keep me on the straight and narrow than the other way around. After spending seven years in the Army, three of those years deployed overseas for active duty, he understands that my edges will always be a little rough. But that doesn't stop him from trying to smooth them out when he can.

Strolling into the grand ballroom, I smile as a swell of pride courses through me. The latest hotel in our chain, Sapphire Resorts, has turned out beautifully, and without a doubt, I believe it's going to be a big success, especially with the location so central to the financial district. *When did I start caring so much about this shit?* I chuckle softly with a small shake of my head and then look for the closest bar. I need a drink if I'm going to get through the next two hours.

I head to the back corner of the ballroom, a spot I know will most likely be a bit quieter, but pause when a flash of gold catches the corner of my eye. I turn my head and draw in a long, appreciative breath as I scan the beauty making her way across the room. Her gaze seems focused on the bar at the front of the room, so I turn my body and casually drift in that direction instead.

As I'm walking, I scan from her gold-clad toes, up her bare, toned legs to mid-thigh, where the hem of her sheer cream dress ends. The sheer fabric is scattered with a thousand different types of golden gemstones that hug her tiny waist and perfect breasts, reflecting against every light in the room. But what really draws my attention is the open back of the dress. Her entire back is bare, exposing skin so smooth, it appears flawless. I clasp and unclasp my hand as I fight the urge to press it flat against her skin as I move closer. It's hard to tell if her hair is long or short because it's all piled on top of her head, as if she knows the power her exposed back possesses.

I stop several feet from the bar and watch as she attempts to cut a path through the mingling throng, waving to try to catch the bartender's attention. The bartender is female; otherwise, I'm certain she would have had a drink in front her before she lifted a single finger.

I continue watching until a rather stout gentleman slides up beside her and attempts to make conversation. It's amusing to watch her try to be kind to the man until I see him reach out and slide his pinky finger down her arm suggestively, a look of disgust crossing her face at the action.

Anger surges through my body, and within seconds, I'm pushing myself between her and the man. A warning snarl slips from my lips as I glare at him and place my hand flat against the center of her back. It feels like silk. It's the single thought that flies through my head before I smile down at her and brush a kiss against her cheek.

"Hello, darling. Are you having a problem getting the cocktails?"

Her wide blue eyes look up at me in surprise and then in knowing relief as she immediately plays into my little game. "Yes! Have you come to rescue me, babe?"

I can't help the wide grin that breaks across my face when she gives me a small wink and mouths silently, "Thank you so much".

"I have." I give her my full attention for only a second, my eyes locking onto hers long enough to see light grey flecks mixed into the blue surrounding her pupil, reminding me of waves churning at sea. I break contact and look at the bartender's name tag.

"Excuse me, Greta?" Whether it's because I'm a somewhat handsome male, or because she realizes a Sapphire is standing in front of her, suddenly, all of her attention is focused on me.

"Yes, sir, what can I get you?" Her cheeks turn a light pink as she fidgets with the bottle opener in her fingers.

I smile warmly to try to settle her nerves, nodding toward the back of the bar. "I'll have a couple fingers of that whiskey, please, on the rocks." I turn my head toward the vision in gold, locking my eyes with hers again. "And, darling, I'm sorry, what did you want again?"

I watch as her eyes narrow and one side of her gloss-lined lips tilt up in a smirk as she tells the bartender that she'll have a Goose on the rocks, her eyes never leaving mine.

Greta sets our drinks down in front of us within seconds, then busies herself with the next person in line. I watch as her delicate fingers, tipped with nails painted black, wrap around the glass and raise it to her mouth, her lips kissing the edge as she draws in a small sip of the clear liquid before slowly lowering it.

"Thanks for rescuing me."

I look down in shock as the hand that was on her back is suddenly cold and empty. I watch her turn and walk away for only a second before I grab my whiskey off the bar and quickly follow, calling after her.

"I'm Ben, in case you were wondering." She stops mid-stride, anchors her foot and then spins around, stopping in front of me, a cocky grin on her face.

"I wasn't. Wondering. But nice to meet you, Ben. Thanks again." She raises the glass in salute and moves to turn again, but I take a step closer as she does, causing her to falter, one eyebrow raising in curiosity. "Yes?"

"You aren't going to tell me your name?" *Jesus, I sound like a desperate idiot who's never seen a beautiful woman before.*

She laughs lightly and takes another sip from her glass, her eyes scanning me from head to toe then pausing briefly at what I'm sure are my tattoos peeking out of my open collar, and then shakes her head. "No, I don't think so."

I rear back in surprise and scoff. "You seriously aren't going to tell me your name?"

She shrugs and challenges me. "Why?"

"Why do I want to know your name?"

She nods and places a hand on her hip, jutting it out slightly as she does. "Yes, why? Are you planning on sending me flowers or are you just trying to get to know me better?" She lifts her glass a little in the air. "Do I owe you because you bought me a drink?"

A little unsure and a lot stunned by her response, I scratch my beard and frown down at her. "You're a spunky little thing, aren't you?"

She lifts her shoulders nonchalantly. "Maybe. Maybe I just know guys like you."

I raise my brows in surprise. "Guys like me?"

She nods and takes her hand off her hip to wave it up and down with a flourish around me. "Yes, guys like you: tall, dark and handsome." She gives me another once over before continuing. "And I'd say rich based on your watch and shoes alone."

I give her my most dazzling smile. "You think I'm handsome?"

A small frown tugs her lips down. "See? That's all you heard. Guys like you think they can throw their pretty little smiles around and we women are just supposed to fall at your feet."

"I wasn't expecting you to fall at my feet. I was just wondering what your name is."

She lifts the glass to her lips again, the ice clinking as she drains the rest of the vodka, and then takes a step closer to hand me the glass. "Like I said, thanks for the drink." She looks me up and down one final time, shakes her head, and then mutters as she turns to leave, "Been there, done that. Not going there again."

Dumbfounded, I watch her walk back through the crowd, her beautiful bare back taunting me as she does. I raise my own glass in response, finishing the whiskey in one swallow. As I lower the glass, I notice Gage, my friend and photographer we hired for the evening, taking some pictures at the edge of the room. I quickly walk back to the bar, deposit the empty glasses, and ask Greta for two beers. Grabbing them, I relocate Gage and make my way over to him.

"Hey, man! How's it going?" I hold one of the beers out to him, which he takes, a grateful look on his face.

"Thanks, man. I need this." He takes a long pull from the bottle. "The shoot is going great. I'm just about done I think. Just want to get some of your brother's speech and then I think I can wrap up."

"Thanks again for filling in last minute. I know Drew really appreciates it."

"No problem at all. It's easy work." He scowls and pulls at the collar of his shirt. "I just wish I didn't have to wear this damn thing. Hate having shit on my neck."

I can't help but chuckle, because I obviously know exactly how he's feeling, but I give him some shit anyway. "Toughen up and quit your bitching."

Gage points to my loosened collar and retorts. "Shut the fuck up! Where the hell is your tie?"

I grin broadly. "I don't work for my brother so I'll wear whatever the hell I want."

We both laugh and take a couple more drinks in silence before Gage points his bottle toward the stage. "Looks like Drew might be getting ready to speak, so I'm going to go find a good spot."

"Okay, look me up after if you want to get another drink." I tip my bottle at him in goodbye and turn to see if I can find Hannah, Drew's wife. Scanning the crowd in front of the stage, I spot her and work my way over, a smile breaking across her face as she sees me, her hand lifting to wave me over.

I wave back and only miss half a beat in my step when I notice the woman in gold is standing next to Hannah, her features a mask of surprise as I approach and kiss Hannah on the cheek. "How's my favorite sister-in-law?"

She kisses me back and giggles. "I'm your only sister-in-law."

"Then you win, hands down." I give her a wink and move to address the three people standing next to her, my eyes landing on my mystery woman, who is shaking her head, a small grin of defeat on her mouth. "Hi, I'm Ben, Hannah's brother-in-law. I don't think we've met before."

"Oh, I'm sorry Ben." Hannah shifts quickly into hostess mode. "This is Drew's friend from college, Mika Kingsley, and his new bride, Reava." She gives me a quick look of apology. "I thought you may have already known him."

"No worries at all, Hannah." I grasp Mika's firm grip in my own and shake it. "Nice to meet you both." I give a warm smile to his wife and then move my attention to the woman on her right, extending my hand, unable to hide the devil in my grin. "And you are?"

She purses her lips and tilts her head, gracefully placing her hand in mine before finally bringing her eyes up to meet mine. "Jill Baldwin. Nice to meet you, Ben."

I've got to hand it to the man; he's very resourceful. His lips curl up into a triumphant smirk. *Damn it.* Of course, he had to be Benjamin freaking Sapphire.

"Jill Baldwin?" He repeats my name, as if he's mulling it over in his head. The timber of his voice travels up my spine, awakening every nerve inside my body. Sex is literally seeping from his pores, and he is one thousand percent the type of guy I need to stay far, far away from. "I know I've heard that name before," he says, not taking his eyes off me.

Dear God, it feels as if he looking right into my inner thoughts. I feel the heat rise in my cheeks. *Nope. Tall, dark, and off limits.* I tell myself sternly. I force myself to get it together.

"I think you were supposed to be at the meeting I had with your brother last week," I reply sweetly. "But you had to cancel last minute?"

"Jill owns that amazing spa downtown, Serenity," Hannah chimes in.

I met with Drew last week after Mika set up the meeting. He thought a partnership with Sapphire Resorts would be a great way for me to expand my business. Quite frankly, I am now happy Ben wasn't at that meeting. I don't think I could have focused. Drew Sapphire is handsome, but his brother—oh my God—that man should be illegal. From his dark hair that's screaming to have my fingers running through it, to the intense gaze in his beautiful hazel eyes, every inch of his impressive six feet is drawing me in, like a moth to a flame. And that is a sure sign that I need to run for the hills, and fast.

"Well, I was sorry to miss the meeting that day, even more so now," he replies smoothly as he flashes me a smile that could melt any pair of panties.

Good God, I need to get away from him. I force a tight smile. "Maybe next time. If you'll excuse me, I need to go powder my nose."

I reach for Rae's arm. "Are you coming?" I ask her urgently.

Raeva raises a brow but nods. She kisses Mika on the cheek. "I'll be back in a bit, love," she tells him sweetly.

My heart is pounding against my chest as if it wants to escape. I take long strides toward the ladies' room, practically dragging poor Rae with me.

"Slow down, Jillybean. These are six-inch heels, ya know?"

I slow my roll. "Sorry, Rae. I just had to get away," I tell her as we step into the fancy bathroom. I look around. The Sapphires really take things to the next level.

Raeva chuckles. "I take it that Ben is tall, dark, and hell no?"

I groan. "I can't possibly do business with Benjamin Sapphire."

Raeva rolls her eyes at me. "Are you seriously going to walk away from a huge opportunity, just because you find a man attractive? I know I don't have to tell you how ridiculous that sounds." She takes a step toward me and places her hand gently on my forearm.

I sigh. "Rae, guys like him—"

"Guys like him?"

"Yeah, too handsome, too rich, too..."

"Too what exactly? Do you realize, you've just pretty much described Mika? And you adore him; I know you do." She smiles widely.

"I adore him because he makes you happier than I've ever seen you."

Rae's face lights up like a Christmas tree. "That he does."

"Benjamin Sapphire is just not what I need in my life right now. I've been down that road plenty of times. I'm not..."

"Whoa, let me stop you right there. We are talking about a business deal, not marriage. If you don't want to date him, then don't.

13

It's that simple."

As usual, my best friend makes total sense. "You're right, I'm being silly." *I am being ridiculous. No matter how gorgeous Ben is, I am in complete control of my actions.* I tell myself, all the while knowing that's not entirely true.

"You good, Jillybean?"

"I'm good."

Raeva folds her arms around me and hugs me. After a beat, I pull away, holding her upper arms, and look at my beautiful bestie. Her long, dark hair is cascading around her shoulders, and her full lips are painted the same red as the silky gown that seems to have been poured onto her. "Have I told you, you look amazing tonight?"

"Repeatedly, but thank you. And, might I add, right back at ya. No wonder you had Ben drooling."

A girlish giggle escapes from my lips. "He was not drooling."

"Oh, please," Rae challenges.

We both are laughing as we walk out of the bathroom. "Is there any particular reason why you keep running off, Jill?"

I almost miss a step. I look up to find Benjamin Sapphire leaning against the wall across from the ladies' room.

"Well, that's my cue," Rae announces as she flashes me a wink.

"Traitor," I mouth at her. I watch her walk away for a moment, an enormous grin on her face, before I turn to face my accuser. "Going to the bathroom is running off?"

I'm surprised with how even my tone is. Judging from the look on Sapphire's face, it's thrown him off, too. But he recovers fast and flashes me a smile as he approaches me.

"So, we can have a drink at the bar then?"

"Look, um, Ben, is it?"

He closes the distance between us and cocks his head. "You know it is."

I bite my lower lip in an attempt to hide my smile; it's fun sparring with him. He's so close now, close enough for me to smell his cologne. Hints of clean soap and earthy scents tickle my nostrils, and it is taking everything I have to stop myself from inhaling deeply. Mercifully, I manage to collect myself. Lifting my head, I look at him and smile sweetly.

"I'm just not that into you."

His eyes sparkle brightly, a twinkle of amusement setting them ablaze. He takes another step closer, his right-hand slipping around my waist, and pulls me against him. It doesn't even occur to me to stop him. Our eyes lock, and I feel his finger trail slowly from my shoulder to the very tip of my index finger. The gentle touch is setting my body on fire. I gasp slightly, screaming inwardly at myself to look away, but my irises are his willing prisoners. My body trembles against his, so close now that I can feel how hard is chest is. He leans in agonizingly slow, and I know that I'm done for. His lips are just mere inches from mine. My eyes flicker to his perfect mouth, and I swallow hard.

"Yes," he whispers against my lips. "I can see just *how little* you are into me." His lips gently brush my cheek and he releases me. The air is thick with desire, and I know it's not just mine. Ben shakes his head, a smirk on his face. "Stubborn little thing, aren't you?"

He takes my hand once more and lifts it to his lips. "I'll definitely be in touch."

And, with those parting words, he leaves me standing there in the hallway, somewhere between feeling bereft and dumbfounded.

BREAKING BENJAMIN

CHAPTER TWO

"When's your next meeting with Jill Baldwin?" I burst into Drew's office and make myself comfortable in one of the wing back chairs in front of his desk. Looking up, I'm met with a look of utter annoyance.

"Well, good morning to you, Benny." He waves his hand to the chair I'm already in. "Won't you come in and have a seat? It's not like I was working on anything." His brow arches high as he finishes, his voice laced with sarcasm. "Can I get you a cup of coffee perhaps?"

"You can get me Jill Baldwin's number," I retort, shaking off his edginess. *He's too wound up for his own good.*

"I'm sorry, whose number do you want?" His fingers are tapping in irritation on his desk.

"Jill Baldwin. Mika's wife's friend. Owns Serenity Spas. You had a meeting with her last week."

Realization dawns and a knowing smile dances on his lips. "Ah, you must have met the lovely Ms. Baldwin at the opening, and now you're interested in a meeting. Am I correct?"

"Did you see her? She's absolutely stunning." I stand from the chair and begin pacing, trying to expend some of the restless energy coursing through my system. "But damn if she isn't playing hard to get."

"Yes, she's hard to miss. I can see why you're taken by her."

I stop and turn in his direction when I hear his fingers cease their movement. "But?" I know there's a but coming. Drew may be my younger brother, but there is no doubt that he's generally the more reasonable one of us.

"But," he gives me a hard stare, "I'm actually quite interested in having her incorporate her spas into our hotels and don't need you to interfere with that."

"So, let me help. If you think it's a good business decision, let me work to make the deal happen."

Drew chuckles and shakes his head. "I think we both know what kind of deal you're interested in when it comes to Ms. Baldwin. Go chase another skirt. This one is too important for you to mess with."

I move to stand in front of his desk and slap my palm down hard. "Damn it, this girl is different! I feel it in my bones."

My brother stands to his full height, which is two small inches taller than me, his blue eyes turning to steel. "Different because she said no? I'm sure that's a new concept for you, big brother."

"Fuck you, Drew." I move to stand next to him to show I'm not intimidated by him in any way. "If memory serves correctly, I don't think it was too long ago that you found yourself in a very similar position. It was only chance that you ran into Hannah that day in the lobby that saved you."

I feel a little badly for shooting below the belt when I see Drew take a step back, his eyes widening in surprise, but the feeling goes away immediately when I hear his consent.

"Fine." He sits back in his seat and types something on his laptop. "I'll text you her information."

"No." Drew's eyes snap to mine in frustration. "I want you to set up another meeting with her, but I'll take the meeting, not you."

He stops typing and looks up at me, anger stewing close to the surface. "So, you're essentially going to trick her into a date with you?"

"No, it's a business meeting, but unfortunately, you aren't going to be able to make it, so I am generously going in your place to ensure discussions move forward." I flash him my cockiest grin and then continue. "Set it up for Thursday, 7 p.m. in the hotel restaurant at the new financial district location."

"A little late for a business meeting, don't you think?" His tone is wry and condescending at best.

"She won't say no to you. You're Drew 'Fucking' Sapphire." This time, I provide him with a genuine smile.

"You got that right." He finally cracks and lets a smile escape before muttering, "You better not screw this up, Benny."

Three long nights later, I stroll into the Blue Ivy and address the hostess. "Good evening. I've got a table reserved under Sapphire."

"Of course, Mr. Sapphire." She takes two menus and leads me to a table. "I have you here, but if you'd prefer something else?"

"Yes, actually." I look toward one of the more private booths along the wall in the back of the room and move in that direction. "I'll take this. Can you show Ms. Baldwin to the table when she arrives, please?"

"Certainly." She sets the menus down and places the wine list in front of me. "Jeffrey will be over in just a moment. Do you need anything in the meantime?"

"No, thank you." I open the wine menu in dismissal and begin browsing the selections. I'm fifteen minutes too early but couldn't stand sitting in my apartment any longer and also wanted the element of surprise when she arrived. I'm generally a whiskey or beer kind of guy, but given this is supposed to be a business meeting, wine seems like the wiser choice.

"Good evening, Mr. Sapphire, sir." A smartly dressed waiter in his mid-thirties stands before me, a white napkin folded neatly over his arm, a black pad at the ready. "I'm Jeffrey and will be your server for the evening. Would you care for something to drink from the bar, or perhaps a bottle of wine?"

"Jeffrey." I open the folder and point to the row of Pinot Noirs. "Let's try one of these bottles. Do you have a recommendation?"

"The 2014 Gap's Crown is very nice. It's from Oregon and has wonderful layers of floral and fruit flavors that aren't overly acidic."

"Great." I close the menu and smile up at him. "Let's do that then."

"Yes, sir." He walks quickly away to retrieve the wine, and I look at my watch for the twentieth time. Six-fifty. I wonder if she'll be prompt, but then consider what she must know is at stake if she goes into business with Sapphire and assume she will be. Jeffrey is back before I can start another thought, twisting and turning the cork off with a soft pop and then handing it to me with a flourish.

I smell it, pretending to know what I'm doing, and nod my head in approval. He pours a small taste into my glass, which I take, swish around, inhale, and taste. My eyebrows fly up as the flavor of the wine bursts across my tongue and slides warmly down my throat. The wine is quite delicious, and I tell Jeffrey just that. He beams as if he had pressed the grapes himself and then pours more into my glass.

I raise my glass for another sip as he steps away, revealing a hidden Jill from his shadow, her lips pressed in a tight line, brows furrowed. Even with a grimace on her face, I cannot help but marvel again at how beautiful she is. My eyes rake over her figure, hugged in a simple form-fitting dress of tan and black, made edgier by the cropped black leather jacket she's wearing. Her feet are also clad in black leather, but with four-inch heels, and she wears only simple diamond studs in her ears.

Standing, I greet her with my most charming smile, my hand extended. "Ms. Baldwin, you're so prompt."

She glares at my hand, ignoring it before responding tartly, "I thought I was meeting with the other Mr. Sapphire."

"Unfortunately, he had an unforeseen emergency and asked me to meet with you instead. He didn't want to cancel on such short notice or stall the discussions for the spas."

"Isn't that convenient?" One well-manicured brow arches sky high.

I chuckle lightly. "For me, perhaps." I move behind her and can't help but notice her eyes following, her neck craning as I place my hands on her shoulders. "Can I take your jacket?"

Seemingly resigned at being stuck with me, she shrugs as I slide the thin, soft material from her shoulders. Her arms are bare, and I notice, very tone and wonder if she works out regularly or if it's great genetics. As I pull the jacket down her arms, I inhale her scent and immediately am reminded of coconuts and the sun. She twirls around, seeming startled to realize she's only inches from me, and takes a sudden step back. "I don't know what game you're trying to play, Ben, but I can assure you right now that this is strictly a business dinner."

God, she's sexy when she's trying to be tough. I give her my most complacent smile and take her elbow, gently guiding her to the table and into the booth before sliding in next to her. "Of course. What else would it be?" I lift the bottle that's been left by Jeffrey. "Wine?"

I really want to take him up on the offer. God knows I could use a drink. But seeing that I am already struggling to string together a coherent thought, adding alcohol in the mix doesn't seem like a smart idea. *Crap, why does he have to be this ridiculously good looking?*

After taking a deep breath to calm my nerves, I immediately regret it. He's sitting right next to me, and the scent of him—clean mixed with woodsy and musky tones—is enveloping me. I can't believe it's *him* that showed up. I regret my choice in clothing; it feels too constricted, too tight. I can literally feel his eyes roaming all over me, like a ghostly touch. I cross my legs and don't miss the fact that his eyes seem glued to the movement, his gaze hoovering at my legs for a long moment before travelling back up to my face. He looks at me expectantly, flashing his pearly whites. Everything about him is drawing me in, and I can't allow that. Alarm bells ring loud inside my head, instantly causing imaginary walls to shoot out of the ground and up to the ceiling.

"I'll stick with water, thank you," I tell him with an eerily calm voice, one that doesn't match what I am feeling at all.

"You don't like wine?"

"Quite the contrary; I love a good glass of wine. But, like I said, this is a business dinner, and I don't mix business with pleasure."

"Ah, so, in your mind, you associate me with pleasure? I will take that as a win for me," he says with a smirk.

I scoff. "I associate you with a few things, Mr. Sapphire. Pleasure isn't on that list, I assure you. I am here to discuss business. If that isn't the case, then I will get up and leave right now."

When I move to do just that, he gently places a hand on my arm. "Listen, I'm sorry," he says sheepishly. "I think we got off on the wrong foot. Can we start over? Please?"

He actually looks contrite and sounds sincere, and I can't help but feel a little bad. I sigh.

"Okay, let's start over," I concede.

He visibly relaxes some, and I tense up more in response. "Ms. Baldwin, thank you for joining me tonight. I know you were expecting my brother, but I assure you that I am just as invested in the company as he is."

I realize it is entirely possible that I am putting too much stock in my belief that this is a set-up. After all, he is a Sapphire and this deal could be lucrative for all parties involved. To think that he would orchestrate this meeting just to get into my pants seems a little arrogant. I mean, I guess I am not unattractive, but that man is sex on legs and can get any woman he wants. Why would he go through all this if it wasn't for business?

I smile at him. "I've been looking forward to the meeting, Mr. Sapphire. I—"

"Please, call me Ben. Mr. Sapphire is my father; I have no desire to be called that."

"Okay... Ben." Just saying his name is causing a tingling feeling in my belly. "And you can call me Jill, if you'd like."

"I'd like."

That earns him a smile. "As I was saying, I have been looking forward to this meeting because I think a collaboration between your resorts and my spa would be a happy marriage."

Ben smiles, and I fight the urge to touch the dimple that appears. He hands me a menu, and I pretend to read it. Instead, I am inwardly trying to collect myself. My heart rate is accelerated, every single nerve ending in my body is at high attention, and my stomach is tied up in a thousand knots. The server approaches the table and asks if we are ready to order. My eyes dart over to Ben, who is studying my expression. I force a smile and nod. I order the first thing I see and honestly, I am not even sure what it was. I hope it is I something that I enjoy eating, because either way, I'm stuck with it now. Ben orders his food, and the server pours us both some water before heading back to put in our food orders.

"My brother tells me that one of the reasons he was so keen to meet you in the first place is the development of your own product line and special services. I understand it's quite revolutionary. Can you tell me more?"

"Of course." I pull my catalog from my attaché, place it on the table, and slide it toward him. I am impressed that he's actually done his homework. He opens it as I tell him about my skincare line, the painless hair removal, and about the special rejuvenating facials we offer. Much to my surprise, he actually hangs on my every word. He seems genuinely interested, asking me follow-up questions and taking notes.

Now that I am talking about my passion, I feel relaxed and in control. I have practiced this speech a million times over, but I am going completely off script. Not because I am nervous, quite contrary really. It flows out of me so naturally, and with my audience of one being so captivated by my words, I dive right in. The food arrives, so I place the catalog back in my attaché and Ben stows his notebook away. Our dinners are placed in front of us, and I'm relieved when I see that I ordered what looks to be a chicken with some kind of sauce. The server pours more wine for Ben and asks me if I would like a glass, too.

"Actually, I'd love a glass," I say with a smile. I expect Ben to comment, but he simply smiles and cuts his steak. I accept the glass from our server and take a sip of the blood red liquid, nearly moaning at the taste. It's delicious. I tell him so and he beams at me.

"This is actually one of my very favorite wines," Ben tells me as the server strides off.

A chuckle escapes my lips.

"That's funny?"

"No, it's just that you don't really strike me as a wine guy."

"That is an astute observation, Ms. Baldwin. What, pray tell, would you say is my poison of choice?"

This is too easy. "Hmmm, that is a hard question." I purse my lips as I pretend to mull it over. "You definitely strike me as a bourbon kinda guy."

Ben raises a brow and a small smile tugs at my lips. "Is that right? What brings you to that conclusion, Ms. Baldwin?"

"I could lie and tell you that I guessed, but I won't. I remember what drink you ordered the night we met." I grin with a little wink.

"You remember what drink I ordered?" His brows arch in feigned delight. "Ms. Baldwin, if I didn't know any better, I would swear that I made an impression on you."

He has no idea. "I'm glad you know better."

His lips curl up into a smile, revealing those dimples of his. I drain my glass and warmth spreads through my belly. I know, though, that it isn't the wine causing this stir inside of me.

"Would you like some more wine?" he asks as he hovers the bottle above my glass.

I am inclined to say yes, because part of me wants to prolong the evening. But a nagging voice in the back of my head is telling me to go. It's telling me that I am setting myself up for disappointment and heartbreak. I need to get off this road. "I think I have had enough. Thank you, Ben," I say with a small smile.

He nods and places the bottle back on the table.

"In fact, I think I should probably call it a night. If you have any more questions, you can email me."

"You're right, it is getting late..." Ben motions the server and requests the check, handing him his credit card without even looking to find out how much the dinner costs. Our server returns swiftly, and Ben puts his credit card back into his wallet. He hesitates for a moment, but then slides out of the booth and picks up my coat. I follow suit and smoothly glide out of the booth. An involuntarily shiver courses through my body as he helps me into it.

"Let me walk you out," he offers. "I'll help you catch a cab."

"Actually, I have a driver waiting for me, but thank you."

"Let me walk you to your car then."

"All right."

We walk through the restaurant, which for the time of night is still very crowded. Ben places his hand on the small of my back, and my breath catches. I notice some longing looks being thrown his way, and I hate to admit that I loathe them. A chilly New York breeze greets us as we step outside onto the teeming sidewalk.

"Well, I think this was a very successful *business* dinner," he tells me as we walk toward my waiting car.

"I think so, too. I am very excited." Upon our approach, the driver gets out of the car and moves to open the door for me, but Ben beats him to it. I get into the back seat and look up at him. "Thank you, Ben."

He presses the button on the window, lowering it before shutting the door. He holds out his hand, and I place mine in it. He brings it to his lips and presses a small, sweet kiss on the back of my hand before letting it go. "Goodnight, Jill."

"Goodnight, Ben," I croak.

Our eyes lock, and even as the driver starts to pull into traffic, I don't look away. He smiles at me, and I give him a small wave. I don't take my eyes off him until we turn the corner. I ride off into the night feeling like I left something behind.

CHAPTER THREE

I walk into the lobby, nod a greeting to the doorman, and stride toward the elevator. "I'm expected."

"Very good, sir." He moves to the phone to alert my presence. "I'll just let them know you're on the way up."

I step into the elevator, press the PH button, and stare at the wall during the thirty second ride until the doors swish open. I walk into the hallway, approach their door, and raise my hand to knock, but it's pulled open before I can connect.

"Benjamin!" A beaming Hannah stands in front of me, Brody placed firmly on her hip, his head leaning on her shoulder, thumb in his mouth. "What brings you over in the middle of the day?" She steps out of the way and motions for me to come inside. "Not that I'm complaining! You know I love seeing you."

I reach for Brody. "Here, let me take him. You look like your arm is going to fall off."

Sighing gratefully, she shifts him from her arms to mine. "He's been a handful these last few weeks. I think it's his molars. He won't let me put him down."

I adjust him so that he's resting with his head down on my shoulder and kiss the top of his downy locks, inhaling and appreciating his baby smell. *Why do they always smell so damn good?* He's like a mini Drew; same dark hair and striking blue eyes. "No Gracie?" I think my favorite part of visiting Hannah is getting to see what kind of witty quips her six-year-old daughter will throw my way.

"School." She turns and starts toward the kitchen. "Come on, you want some coffee?"

"Sure, that sounds great." I follow her, stepping over toys along the way, and sit on a stool while she moves around prepping the coffee for us.

"You hungry?" She walks to the fridge and pulls the door open. "I can make you a sandwich or a salad if you want?"

"Just coffee is great." I smile at her and think how lucky my brother is to have someone this loving in his life. Although their beginning was definitely a little unconventional, nothing about their life today is. They share a love and devotion for each other that I can't help but admire and hope myself to find. I'm thirty-six years old, almost thirty-seven. I'm getting tired of the chase, nameless girls, and my empty apartment.

"So, you going to tell me what's on your mind?" She lifts a brow as she sets a big mug in front of me, steam rising from the hot, black liquid.

I take a sip and grin. "What, you think I have a motive? Just couldn't stop by to see my favorite sister?"

"I see you almost every day, Ben." She comes up beside me and pulls a now sleeping Brody out of my arms, and I watch as she places him gently in a nearby pack-n-play before walking back to sit on the stool beside mine. "That's how I know you've got something on your mind."

I smile sheepishly into my coffee before looking back up at her. "Guilty as charged I guess."

"All right, spill then." She pulls her cup of coffee closer and takes a sip.

"There's a girl." Before I can get another word out, she starts laughing. My brow scrunches up in confusion at her response.

She slaps her hand over her mouth and shakes her head as she gets her laughing under control. "It's Jill Baldwin, isn't it?" My eyes open wide, and she smacks her hand on the counter when she registers my surprised look. "Uh-huh! I knew it! I saw the way you looked at her at the opening celebration!" She hits her hand on my leg this time and smiles wide. "I told Drew there was something there, and he played dumb. I knew it! You like her, don't you?"

I cock my head and nod. "I do."

"I knew it!" She claps her hands in delight and beams like she just won the lottery. Women are strange. "Okay, what can I do to help?"

"She's playing hard to get, and let's face it, Hannah, you wrote the book on that one."

Her mouth falls open as her brows shoot up. "Benjamin Sapphire, I did not play hard to get. My situation was completely different and you know it."

"Okay, if you say so." I raise a brow in doubt. "The point is, she says everything is about business and insists on keeping things that way, but there is a chemistry there. When we're together, talking, just being in the same space, it's different than anything else I've ever felt before, and I know she feels it, too. But, damn it, she's fighting it tooth and nail."

"Is it just the fact that she's saying no?" She raises her hand to stop me from talking. "Don't get mad at the question; it's a fair one. I mean, let's face it, Ben, you don't hear that word very often."

I roll my eyes. "I hear it more than you think, and no, that's not the issue. Because you're right; for every one person that says no, there are ten that say yes."

"Well, aren't you just special, little lover boy?" She's joking when she says it, but what she doesn't realize is that it's not a title I want. I can't remember the last time I spent an actual night with anyone and felt happy about it the next morning, or had a conversation with a woman that intrigued me. Most of the time, women approach and proposition me, and spending every night by yourself gets lonely. It fills a void but definitely not anything in my heart. I think she realizes she's hit a nerve because she reaches over and grabs my hand. "I'm sorry, Ben. I was only joking. You are one of the most caring men I've ever met in my life. Let's not forget that I know this better than almost anyone."

She's referring to her first husband, Jackson, who was killed in action shortly after I lost my leg. Losing him and two other brothers-in-arms was almost more than I could bear, especially while I was dealing with the loss of half my leg. With help, though, I did get through the losses and started a gym for disabled Vets. It's free and there for anyone that needs its services. It's named after her late-husband.

I squeeze her hand and force a smile. "I know."

"So, we need to figure out how to get Jill to take you seriously." She taps her finger on her chin, thinking, and then suddenly sits up straight and points her finger in the air. "I know what you need to do!"

"Okay, let's hear it." I can't wait to see what she's come up with.

"Well, you are definitely interested in her business, right? And, that seems to be the most important thing to her at the moment, right?"

"Definitely a top priority for her. And, yes, me too. It would actually be a great partnership." I waggle my brows. "In every way if I can help it."

She rolls her eyes. "Oh, Benny."

I frown at her use of Drew's nickname for me. "Keep going."

"Then you need to go check out her business. You can use it as an in to see her again. Go to her spa, say you want to see and experience the services in person. You need her to first believe that you're committed to the business partnership before she's ever going to take a chance on you personally."

"That's it?" It seems to simple.

"Yes, that's it." She reaches for her phone, brings up a number, and then puts the phone to her ear after pressing call.

"Hey, Jill! It's Hannah Sapphire. How are you?" She's silent for a minute, nodding her head as she listens to Jill. "Yes, I had a great time at the opening, as well. I was so glad you were able to come. I was actually wondering if you could help me out with something?"

She gets up and walks back and forth in the kitchen as she talks. "Drew and his brother Ben have worked so hard getting the resort up and running, and I was hoping to treat them to some services at your spa. They need to relax for a bit!"

She's nodding her head again. "Yes, you are so right! It's a wonderful way for them to see first-hand what you do!" She nods her head a few more times and then gives me a big thumbs-up. "Yes, I can get them there on Thursday for you. Not a problem at all. Thank you so much. Let's get together ourselves soon, too! You, me, and Raeva for lunch! Okay, bye, Jill!"

Ending the call, she looks up at me with a victory grin on her face. "Step one of Operation Get Jill is complete! You and Ben have a full spa package scheduled for this Thursday at noon!"

I smile brightly back at her and wrap her in a hug. "You are the best! Thanks!"

––––––––––

Two days later, Drew and I walk into Serenity at exactly ten minutes 'til noon for our appointment. "This was a good idea, brother. The best way for us to determine just how top of the line their products and services are."

"You have your wife to thank for this, not me. She came up with the brilliant idea."

"Ah, yes, the 'Operation Get Jill' plan. Hannah did mention that. I'm trying to forget about that part of this visit."

I grin over at him. "But that's the best part of the whole afternoon." Our conversation pauses as we're greeted at reception and then shown to a locker room where we can change. I thought Jill was going to meet us, so I voice my disappointed to Drew when I don't see her.

"I'm sure she's quite busy. Perhaps she got pulled into something else. Besides, we're here for several hours. I'm sure we'll see her at some point."

We're led to a medium sized room where two massage tables are set up. Two women are waiting in the room and smile when we enter, one of them speaking. "Good afternoon, gentlemen. Jill booked this room for you, in case you wanted to discuss business during your massage, but if you'd prefer a single room, we can accommodate that for you as well."

I look at Drew, and we both shrug in unison. "This is fine."

"Wonderful. We'll step out and let you get situated on the table. Just slide under the sheet, and we'll start face down."

The women leave and we both move to a table. I sit on the table before removing my robe, bend down and pull my prosthetic off below the knee, then lean it against the table. Drew's already sliding under the sheet as I stand and balance on one leg to take my robe off and then slide under my own. The room is warm, and soft melodic music is playing over speakers hidden somewhere. It's relaxing, and I chalk one point up for Jill and her business.

"So, do you really like her, or is it just the thrill of the chase?" Drew asks from his side of the room, his words slightly mumbled as his face is lying sideways on the table.

"It's not the chase." I scoff. "Well, you know, a little chase is always fun, but that's not it. Yes, she absolutely may be one of the most beautiful woman I've laid eyes on, but it's more than that. There's a spark there. She's challenging and smart and isn't afraid or intimidated by me one little bit. It's refreshing to find a woman who is utterly sure of herself and what she wants but also shows some vulnerability."

The door clicks open, and I hear two sets of feet shuffle quietly in. "Any objection to oils?" one of the women asks. Drew and I both grunt out a, "No." I feel the sheet being adjusted and then a slight gasp as all movement stills for a minute. I'm never sure if it's because of the tattoos covering my back or if it's my leg, but the pause is so short, and I'm so used to it by now, that I dismiss it as quickly as it occurred.

"So, are you going to ask her on a real date?" Drew mumbles between a moan.

I feel oil on my back and then let out a long sigh myself when hands start to work my shoulders. I boxed for two hours yesterday, and I'm sore as hell today.

"That's the plan." I groan as the fingers dig hard into a knot on my back. "But, first, I think I have to get her to admit she likes me."

Jill 15 minutes earlier...

I could have killed Anna a few minutes ago. Rationally, I know it isn't her fault that the daycare called to inform her that Casey—her little girl—has a fever, and thus per policy, needs to be collected from daycare. I know she had no intention of leaving me high and dry. But still, I can't help but feel annoyed that she put me in this situation, today of all days.

The spa is completely booked, and I have no other available staff. Seeing as today is all about impressing the Sapphire men, I have no other choice but to step in myself. We walk back into the room after a few minutes have passed by. Aisha asks if they object to oils, and neither does. She has already positioned herself beside Drew and started his massage. *I should have insisted before that she did Ben.* I begrudgingly think to myself.

I gently pull back the sheet, and a small gasp escapes from my lips. Never in my life have I ever seen someone's back and thought it was sexy. But this man's back is a work of art—all muscle and sun-kissed skin decorated with ink. My eyes roam freely over his exposed back. I knew he had tattoos but would have never imagined that so many graced his skin. At first glance, I think it's just a tribal tattoo, but upon further inspection, I find several animals sketched into his back. The large wolf particularly grabs my attention, and I long to trace my fingers over the fur that looks so real.

Grabbing a few bottles from the warmer, I mix the different oils together in my hands. I smooth the oil all over his broad shoulders and his back, tracing each muscle. I've never really been a tattoo kinda girl, but his are beautiful, not to mention the canvas. I am so enthralled that I nearly miss when Drew mumbles something about asking "her" out on a real date. My heart rate accelerates and begins to knock against my ribcage as my fingers kneed his firm flesh. *Is he talking about me?*

"That's the plan," he says as my fingers make short work of a knot in his back. He groans, and the sound of it causes a stir in my belly. He tells Drew that he has to get "her" to admit she likes him. And, I know then, without a shadow of a doubt, that he is talking about me. Frankly, it annoys me, and not just because he is cocky enough to think that I might have more feelings for him than I am letting on. Mostly, it's because I know that his cocky self is right, even though I don't want him to be. Drew chuckles.

"How are you planning to pull that off, Romeo? It's not like your charms have worked on her so far."

I bite my bottom lip to stifle my laugh. Drew is funny.

"What do you know?" he grumbles in response. He sounds sullen, and it is adorable. My hands continue to explore, and I have a hard time keeping my inner dialog under control. As my fingers sweep across his back and dip lower to his buttocks, I nearly groan myself. It's rare for a man to have a nice backside, but Ben? Yeah, the man wrote the book on having a great ass. I tell myself to focus. You'd think I've never done this before.

I pull the sheet back up to his shoulders and position myself at the bottom of the table. I'm about to lift the sheet when I notice a prosthetic leg leaning against the table. I cock my head, glancing at the table beside me, but neither Drew nor Aisha is paying attention to us. I lift the sheet to position it so his lower half is exposed and see that it's indeed Ben's prosthetic. I had no idea that he had lost part of his leg.

Shaking my head, I attempt to clear my thoughts, as if my head is an etch-a-sketch. I rub some more oil onto my hands and start to massage his upper legs. He stiffens for a short moment when I slide my hands near his stump but soon relaxes under my fingers.

Maybe, I have been judging him unfairly? Maybe, my opinion of him has more to do with my own fears? Maybe, I should just give the man a chance? I have been trying so hard to keep him at arm's length, to deny—even to myself—that there is an obvious attraction between us. But, honestly, I am not sure I can muster up the will to deny it anymore.

"You know what?" Ben says.

"What?" Drew mumbles.

"I'm just gonna ask her."

Drew lifts his head toward Ben and opens his eyes. His eyes pop wide when his gaze lands on me, a smirk appearing on his face. I wasn't expecting that, and my eyes widen.

"You are just going to ask her what, Benny?"

I smile back at Drew and shake my head.

"I'm just going to lay it on the table."

"You are laying on a table."

"You know what I mean, asshole," he says, clearly a little irritated. "If I go to her and just tell her how I feel, ask for a chance to get to know her better over dinner or something, what else can she say besides yes?"

My brow shoots up, and Drew looks at me expectantly. I pull the sheet back and cover him up then make my way toward the head of the table. I lean in close until my mouth is right by his ear. "I'll tell you what else she can say. I'm not your typical kinda girl. I expect gentleman-like behavior—open doors, pull out my chair type of thing. If you are running late, pick up a phone and call or don't bother showing up. If you can live with that, you can pick me up tomorrow night at seven," I tell him.

I stand straight and walk toward the door, just as Ben pushes himself up on the table. I reach for the handle but pause briefly. "Oh, and Ben? Any man that wants to take me out to dinner has to bring me flowers. White lilies are my favorites, if you care."

Ben stares up at me, shock apparent on his face for only a second before he flashes me a stunning smile. "White lilies, huh?"

I smile and nod.

"Duly noted."

After I leave the room, I scurry to my office to catch my breath, or at least until my heartbeat slows down. I need a minute or two just to collect my thoughts. The Sapphire men are scheduled to be here for most of the afternoon, but luckily for me, I can hide in here while my staff takes over. That massage was intense, and I cannot believe I agreed to go out with him. Trying to focus on work for a while, I get some done, but thoughts of Ben, his very naked body, and a date with him tomorrow keep distracting me.

38

I need some girl time to help me collect my thoughts. I pull my cellphone out and go to the group text between myself, Rae, and Mik and tell them that I need an emergency cocktail meeting tonight. I press send and impatiently await their responses when a knock on my door distracts me.

"Yes?" I call out to my closed door.

The door opens, and Sage, the front desk girl, sticks her head in. "Hey Jill?"

"Yes?"

"There is a delivery for you."

"Okay. Do I need to sign for it or something?"

"Um, no, but I think you might want to come and see this."

I rise to my feet and walk toward the door but step back when it opens wider and several delivery people enter, and begin filling up my office with white freaking lilies. A girlish giggle escapes my lips as my cheeks heat up and flush a light pink. The last person to walk in is holding a bouquet so large that I don't notice it's Ben until he places the flowers on top of my desk.

"I see that you don't half-ass things then," I say with a small chuckle.

He smirks and waves a hand across my flower-filled room. "Go big or go home?"

"That is a dangerous precedent you are setting for yourself, Mr. Sapphire," I tell him playfully.

"I'm okay with that," he tells me as he leans closer. "I think you're worth it."

I'm smiling so big, my face hurts. I've got to hand it to the man. He is good.

"I'd like to properly ask you out." He looks at me, brow raised, an expectant look on his handsome face.

"By all means," I retort playfully.

He flashes me those dimples of his, and I already know I am a goner. "Ms. Baldwin, I'd love to take you out for dinner tomorrow night if you are free?"

"It's kind of last minute. I will have to check my schedule," I deadpan, glancing around the large bouquet of flowers to glance at my calendar.

"Of course," he says thoughtfully.

"Hmmm," I tell him. "I think I might be able to squeeze you in."

We both smirk at one another, and he takes a step forward.

"Does seven work for you?" he asks.

"It does." I walk to my desk, jot my address and cell number down on my business card, and then stroll back to hand it to him.

Ben leans in and places a gentle kiss on my cheek as he slides the card from my fingers. I close my eyes and let out a sigh as his lips make contact with my cheek. "See you tomorrow night, Jill."

"Looking forward to it, Ben."

He turns to leave my office.

"Oh, and Ben?"

He stops walking and turns to face me.

"Thank you for the flowers. Nice touch," I say with a wink.

He just flashes that sexy grin and nods his head once before striding out. And I am in no way ashamed to admit that I watch his glorious backside until he has sauntered out of sight.

CHAPTER FOUR

The town car pulls up in front of her building precisely five minutes 'til seven, and I realize I'm nervous. I can't remember the last time I felt nervous; well, at least, about picking a woman up for a date. There were plenty of times overseas that I was more than nervous, but those were life and death situations. This is definitely not that. I take a deep breath and tell the driver I'll be just a minute.

I step out of the car and approach her building but stop in my tracks, my heart skipping two beats in my chest as I see her exit the building. Did I just say this isn't a life or death situation? Because what she's wearing literally takes my breath away. She sashays up to me, hips swaying lightly back and forth as her heels click on the pavement, her smile brightening the dusky night sky.

I sweep my gaze up her body, clad in a little black dress, but not your typical LBD. Oh, no, not my Jill. This one hugs every curve of her body, starting with the high neckline that is followed by two, black sheer strips; the second strip revealing just a peek of her cleavage. The dress falls a few inches above her knees, but there's a slit in one side of the skirt that exposes almost her entire thigh with each step. She's teasing me, and the smile she's giving me says she knows it.

She comes to a stop in front of me, and I reach out and gently clasp her hand in mine, raise it to my lips, and brush a soft kiss against her knuckles. "You look exquisite."

Her cheeks flush just the lightest color of pink as she casts her eyes down to my feet and then leisurely up my body until she meets my gaze. "You look pretty fine yourself, Mr. Sapphire."

I grimace at being called Mr. Anything but don't want to start the evening off on the wrong foot, so I smile and nod my head in thanks. "I would have come up."

"I was ready. No need." She fidgets with her small clutch and smiles. "Am I dressed appropriately? You didn't say where we were going?"

"You're perfect." I move my hand to her elbow and guide her to the town car where the driver is already waiting with an open door. I help her in and then move around to the other side of the car, settling myself in beside her. As soon as I sit in the enclosed space with her, I'm assaulted by her smell and have to close my eyes for a minute to try to identify the scent. It's unique and not the overly sweet perfume other women often wear. This is light and fresh and reminds me of how the air smells in the forest after a summer storm.

"Are you okay?" Her voice is a bit timid.

My eyes fly open, and I turn my head so I can meet her gaze. "I was smelling you."

"Smelling me?" Her brows furrow in confusion.

"Yes." I lean my head forward so that my nose is almost touching her neck, and I inhale deeply. I lift my gaze back to her, not pulling away. "You smell like the rain, clean and crisp and pure."

Her hand moves to her neck as she pulls back from me just a bit, and I realize I might be invading her space a little too closely so I pull myself back up straight. "Sorry. I didn't mean to make you uncomfortable."

Her hand moves from her neck and drops down onto mine as she provides me with a warm smile. "You aren't making me uncomfortable. It's a nice compliment. Thank you."

I turn my hand so I can grasp her fingers in mine, pulling it into my lap, my thumb sweeping back and forth across her palm. Her skin is soft and warm against mine. "You're welcome."

"So, are you going to tell me where we're going?" She tilts her head to one side as she asks.

"You don't like surprises?" I raise an eyebrow in response.

"Only good surprises."

"This is a good one. I promise."

She chuckles. "Already making promises?"

I frown. "Is that a bad thing?"

"Only when you don't deliver, and in my experience, I've learned most men don't."

Immediately feeling challenged by her statement, I raise my brows. I grasp her hand a little tighter and yank her flush to me, a yelp of surprise escaping her painted red lips which are now a breath away from mine. I take her face gently in my other hand and meet her hard stare.

"Let me assure you, Jill, I'll deliver on any promise I make to you. And I also guarantee you won't be disappointed because I'm not like most men, and I don't like being compared to them. Understand?"

My voice is just short of a growl, but she doesn't look scared. She looks aroused. Her breath is falling in short little pants, and her gaze keeps moving from my eyes to my mouth, her pink tongue darting out to run across her lips as she nods. "Got it."

I move my hand slightly and run my thumb over the same trail her tongue just took, her breath inhaling sharply as I do, her eyes fluttering shut. I lean in, but instead of kissing her and doing the expected, I brush my nose across her cheek, down her neck, and then up to her ear, brushing against her soft locks and finally whispering, "I could kiss you right now. I want to. So badly. But in *my* experience, really good things are worth the wait."

She pulls back sharply from my grasp and purses her lips, fire burning in her eyes. "You, Benjamin Sapphire, are a tease."

I give her my most devilish grin. "And you, Jill Baldwin, are fun to tease." Her mouth falls open to respond, but I point out the window and speak. "We've arrived, and just in the nick of time, I think."

"Just in the nick of time for you, I think," she retorts.

I step out of the car and motion for the driver to stay as I move to the other side to open Jill's door. "Is there a restaurant in this marina?" I watch as she swivels her head back and forth in search of one.

"Sort of." I take her hand and start toward one of the docks where a large yacht is moored. "Come on, it's this way."

"Are we going on that?" She points to the boat, eyes wide.

I'm thrilled to have surprised her and maybe even a little proud that I can share such a luxurious experience with her. The yacht is actually my parents', but they rarely use it these days and were more than happy to lend it to me, as well as the staff, for the evening. Especially after they found out that I'd be taking a date on board. I think, they're afraid I'm never going to settle down. "We sure are. Do you like boats?"

"Um, sure. I mean, this is more than a boat. But are you sure I'm really dressed for this?" She pulls back on my hand, stalling our forward progress.

I chuckle at her dress concerns. "Jill, this is a luxury yacht. You won't have to do any mooring or sailing on this. You're absolutely perfect."

"So, we're actually going to leave the dock and go out on the water?" Her voice rises an octave.

"Yep." I start moving forward again. "The staff have a wonderful dinner they're preparing for us, and we can relax and watch the stars as we eat and take in the New York City skyline."

"That sounds wonderful. I've never been on a luxury yacht before."

I help her onto the yacht and lead her to the main salon where the staff are waiting. Introductions are made before the captain excuses himself to get our trip underway. Heather, one of the attendants, pours us each a glass of champagne, and I usher Jill toward the deck.

"Isn't it beautiful?" I want to make sure she's comfortable, but I also am doing my damndest to try to impress this woman.

"It really is gorgeous. It feels so decadent." She wraps her arms around herself and shivers as we approach the railing. I shrug my jacket off and drop it over her shoulders as I move to stand behind her and shield the wind.

"Is it too cold for you? We can go back inside." I run my hand lightly down her arm to warm her.

"No, it's fine. I like the fresh air." She turns her head and gives me a smile. "Thank you for your jacket."

"Let me know if you get too cold. I can get you a blanket." I step closer to her so the heat of my body is against hers. She leans back against me and lets out a long sigh, which in turn makes my heart race.

45

I want her to feel relaxed with me, comfortable. I want this to be one of the best nights of her life and feel like we're off to a perfect start.

"Is it too cold for you? We can go back inside," Ben asks with concern in his voice as he gently rubs my arms on either side, trying to warm me.

Oh, God, please no.

I tell him I am fine and that I am enjoying the fresh air; at least, it's not entirely a lie. I turn my head to face him and smile. When I thank him for his jacket, he offers to get me a blanket if I get too cold. He's very sweet, and I hate that this date is probably going to be ruined by my seasickness. I am inwardly kicking myself, knowing I should have spoken up when I had the chance. Now, I have to put on my big girl panties and power through. He steps closer, pressing his body against mine. I am a little taken aback by how natural this feels, but I don't dwell and let myself enjoy the moment. I lean back against him, and a soft contented sigh falls from my lips. With my head resting against his chest, I listen to his heart beating. It's accelerated, like mine. Ben leans in and kisses the top of my head. I lift my gaze, and his eyes fix on mine. We stare at each other for a moment. Suddenly, he spins me around and pushes my back against the railing, caging me with one arm and holding my face with the other.

"Fuck waiting," he breathes out.

His lips crash down on mine, gentle little pecks at first but that just won't do for me. I throw my arms around his neck, the jacket slipping from my shoulders. But, right now, I don't even care. I deepen the kiss, and while it starts off sweetly, our tongues dancing around each other, exploring, tasting each other, it soon turns more frantic, almost desperate. Any feeling of nausea or cold is forgotten as this man gloriously invades my mouth. My entire body feels like it is on fire, and the heat between my thighs is almost unbearable. There is no denying that I want him. *Right now*. We are interrupted by the clearing of a throat and both turn to face a very obviously embarrassed member of staff, whose name currently escapes me.

"I am so sorry, Mr. Sapphire. I wanted to let you know that dinner is being served."

Ben apparently recovers way faster than I do, because he flashes her a smile and thanks her. He holds out his hand to me, and I take it without a shred of hesitation. I'll follow him anywhere right now. We head inside, and I nearly gasp when I see the fabulous spread before us. The table is beautifully set, and the food smells delicious. I can't disguise the smile beaming from my face when I notice the vase of white lilies on the center of the table. Ben pulls out my chair and I lower myself in to it. He makes his way across from me and gracefully drops into his seat, flashing that smile that makes me weak in the knees, and I am happy that I am sitting down. The girl that caught us making out on the deck walks back in with our plates of appetizers, and I feel my cheeks heating when her gaze meets mine. She smiles at me sweetly and gives me a wink, causing me to chuckle. Ben raises his brow in question, but I just shake my head.

"This looks beautiful," I tell him.

"That it does," he replies, eyes fixed on me.

That earns him a smile. I place my napkin on my lap, and just as

I am about to take a bite, the boat rocks and a wave of nausea overtakes me. I can feel my stomach contents coming up, and my eyes widen and flash over to meet his. Panicked, I scan the room, trying to search for a bathroom. I can't see myself right now, but I am convinced that I must be positively green at this moment.

"Bathroom," I gasp.

Ben jumps out of his chair and is over to me in a heartbeat. He lifts me into his arms and carries me swiftly into the bathroom. I can't even worry about him being here as I drop to my knees in front of the toilet. Ben kneels beside me and holds my hair as the first wave from my stomach makes its appearance. I am absolutely mortified, but I am unable to stop the tsunami that is washing over me. Ben is holding my hair with one hand and stroking my back with the other. When it finally feels as if the sickness is letting up some, embarrassment rears its ugly head. I cover my mouth with my hand and stand, stumbling toward the sink. After I turn on the faucet and rinse out my mouth, I look up and grimace when I see my reflection in the mirror.

"Did you know you get seasick?" he asks me.

I bite my lip as our eyes meet in the mirror and I nod.

"Then why would you let me take you out on a yacht?"

I feel contrite.

"I'm so sorry to have ruined our date. I didn't want to ruin our evening by complaining about where you chose to take me. When I saw how much effort you had put into tonight, I didn't have the heart to, but I went and ruined it any way."

Ben makes his way over to me, positions himself behind me, and wraps his arms around my waist.

"I am so sorry that you feel sick, Jill. I am truly sorry." He leans in and kisses the top of my head. "I should have asked you specifically if you enjoyed being on the water."

I nod once more and he smiles.

"Give me a second to get this vessel turned around," he tells me.

"Okay," I mutter.

He smiles and asks me if I will be okay for a moment, and I tell him I'll be fine. He comes back only a short moment later and wraps a blanket around me before he leads me back onto the deck. We sit in complete silence with his arm draped around me. I am grateful when we make it back to the dock so quickly. We thank the staff, and Ben wastes no time ushering me off the boat and onto the dock. My legs are still a little wobbly, and he must notice, because he lifts me into his arms and carries me to the waiting town car. The driver sees us coming and opens the door for us. Ben gently deposits me into the car and straps me in before walking around and sliding into the seat next to me.

"Will you give me a chance to redeem myself?" he asks me sweetly.

I look at the man that just held my hair as I lost every last bit of what was in my stomach, and am overcome with an unfamiliar feeling. Not able to put any words together at this moment in time, I just nod.

CHAPTER FIVE

Frustration reigns supreme as I walk around the car to climb in beside Jill. Have I made her feel so uncomfortable that she couldn't share the truth with me about her aversion to being on the water? Reasonably, I know she was only trying to make the best out of what ended up being a bad predicament for her, but I want her to feel she can be completely open with me and know I won't be upset.

I open the door and lower myself into the seat next to her. One look in her direction has me doing a complete one-eighty. She's practically curled herself up like a kitten, the blanket from the yacht wrapped around her, making her tiny form somehow look even smaller. Her eyes are downcast, her skin still so pale from the turbulence her body felt on the boat. She musters a small smile and peeks up at me from under her dark lashes. "I'm so sorry, Ben. I should have said something."

Not wanting her to feel one ounce of remorse over any time we spend together, including this disaster of a date, I slide closer and unbuckle her seat belt. I gather her in my arms and pull her into my lap and up against my chest. "Please, no apologies. I understand you were only trying to brave it out to please me."

Her head bobs up and down against my shirt, her soft hair tickling the exposed portion of my chest. And, yes, I inhale again, because even though she was sick only a short time before, she still smells lovely.

"Will you give me a chance to redeem myself?" I whisper gently against the top of her head.

She nods again and snuggles her body into mine, resting her head against my shoulder.

"Dinner tomorrow? At my place? I'll cook for you, and I promise, I live on solid ground."

She nods again but then stops abruptly. "I actually have plans tomorrow night, but I can do the night after if you're free."

"I am now." I pull her petite frame tighter against me and drop another kiss on top of her head. I hate that she's feeling so terrible and that it's my doing. I guess I'll have to make sure I do a little recon work for our next date—find out what she likes and doesn't like to eat, and any allergies she may have. I am not going to put her in a position again where she feels like she may disappoint me.

The car comes to a slow stop as it pulls up outside of her building. The driver jumps quickly out of the car and opens my door for me. Jill moves to get off my lap, but I move my arms under her legs and pull her flush to me. "I've got you."

I turn and place both feet on the pavement and thank God I've strengthened my one good leg so it's strong enough to rise out of the car with her in my arms. She looks up at me, her eyes soft, her color finally returning to the lovely shade of pink it should, the corners of her perfect lips lifting just slightly. "Thank you for taking care of me, Benjamin."

What I really want to do is crush my mouth against hers, but instead, I brush a soft kiss against her forehead and smile. "Nothing gives me greater pleasure." And I truly mean it when I say it.

The door to her apartment is open before I even reach it, a look of concern on the doorman's face. "Is Ms. Baldwin ill? Can I do anything?"

"She'll be just fine. Just an upset stomach. Can you get the elevator for us?" I stride in its direction, the doorman scurrying ahead of me to push the call button.

"Ms. Baldwin, you just ring down if you need anything. James or myself will run out."

"You're so sweet, Henry. Thank you." She smiles weakly as we pass by and into the elevator that has arrived.

I nod my head in thanks to Henry, and then look at Jill. "You okay to stand? I'll put you down if so."

She nods her head, so I lower her legs to the floor but keep one arm firmly around her waist to keep her close. "What floor?"

"Penthouse."

My brows rise in surprise as I lean forward and stretch my hand out to push the PH button.

"It's not like that. Really. I share it with Mikaela Kingsley," she says defensively.

"I didn't say a thing." But now it all makes sense. Mikaela is filthy rich, and one of the sweetest women on the planet. I'm happy to know she's living in good company.

"I saw the look on your face when I said penthouse," she retorts sharply.

Ah, she's definitely feeling better. Her spark is slowly igniting back to life, and this makes me smile down at her in relief. "That was simply surprise. No judgement."

"Well, I hope not. I've worked really hard for what I have. Mik has been a godsend and one of my best friends."

Unable to help myself, I bend down and peck a kiss on the very tip of her nose. "I agree. Mikaela is one of the very best people I know."

This seems to placate her, because she just nods her head tightly and then leans against my shoulder. I seriously wish I could hold her against me all night, but know I need to put her needs first right now. The elevator comes to a stop and we step out into the foyer. There are two penthouse suites on the floor so I turn and look at her. "Which door, Jill?"

"Oh, sorry, that one." Her delicate hand snakes out from the blanket, and a finger points to the door on the left. I lead us in that direction and am about to ask her for the key, when the door swings open, Mikaela standing in the entrance.

"Jill! What happened?" She glances to her friend and then up at me with an accusatory expression on her face. "What did you do to her, Benjamin Sapphire?"

I'm about to speak my defense, but Jill beats me to it. "He's been wonderful, Mik. I just got a bit seasick."

Mik slaps my arm and then places her hands on her hips. "You took her on a boat? Are you crazy?"

I let out a sigh an in attempt to not lose my temper. "Can you step aside so we can come in?"

"Oh!" Her eyes pop wide as she realizes she's standing in the middle of the doorway and steps aside. "Sorry."

I lift one brow and frown as I walk past her, Jill still pressed to my side. "And I had no idea she got seasick. She didn't tell me until *after* the boat left the shore and got sick." I stop and turn my head toward a trailing Mik. "I would never have put her in a position to make her ill if I had known." I continue further into the apartment.

I look down at Jill and soften my voice. "Which way to your room love?"

She tilts her head to one side of the room. "Down that hallway. It's the second door on the left, but, Ben, I'm okay now. I'm feeling much better."

"I've got you." I don't care how uncomfortable she might feel right now; I'm not letting her go until I know she's safe in her room. I follow the direction she's given and guide her into the bedroom. Mik's still trailing behind me and flicks on the light, then runs around me so she can pull back the covers on the bed. I gently place Jill on the bed and slide my arm out from around her waist.

She smiles up at me and trails her hand down my arm as it moves away from her, finding my hand and giving it a squeeze. "Thank you, Ben. Even though things didn't go quite as planned, you've been wonderful."

I lean forward, wrap my free hand around the back of her head, and pull her forward until my lips press against her forehead in a quick kiss. "I promise, our next date will be one thousand times better."

"I can't wait," she whispers back.

We release each other as I rise and turn to find Mik watching us like a hawk. Before she can squawk at me again, I raise my finger to silence her. "Just take care of her." Then, I stroll past her and out of the apartment.

"Good date then?" Mikaela asks, amused as she sits on the bed next to me.

I dramatically bury my head into the pillow and groan loudly, much to her amusement. "Glad that my misery is entertaining to you."

Mikaela pats me on the head. "I'm sorry, babe. I promise I'll try to glee over your misery later when you feel better."

"Geez, thanks."

I stand and head to the bathroom so I can change and brush my teeth, but both our heads snap to the door, which is thrown open as Raeva bursts in. "What the heck happened?" she demands.

Rae looks incredible; she and Mika must have been on a date themselves. That man is always thinking of ways to sweep her off her feet.

"Well?" she urges as she lowers herself on the bed with Mik, watching as I grab pajamas from a drawer and walk into my attached bathroom. I can hear them loud and clear as I change and brush my teeth.

"He took her on a yacht," Mikaela explains.

"Is he crazy?" Raeva belts out.

"My exact response to him."

Mikaela says, laughing, "Girl, when we got back from dinner and James told us that you were carried in the building looking like a ghost, I nearly had a conniption! I left Mika standing in the lobby and ran into the elevator! Ugh, I could kill Ben right now! What the heck was he thinking?"

"He didn't know. It's not his fault," I protest as I walk back into the room. "I swear, guys, he was amazing. So sweet. He held my hair and stroked my back and even carried me to the car. Ben really was the perfect gentleman."

I look up when there is a lack of response and find my two besties gaping at me.

"Jillian Baldwin, are you swooning?" Rae teases.

I roll my eyes.

"Don't deny it, you totally are," Mik chimes in.

I sigh. What's the point in denying? My flushed cheeks have already betrayed me. "He asked me out again," I admit shyly.

"Tell us everything," the say in unison. "And don't you dare leave anything out!"

I can't help the smirk that appears on my face when I start to talk about Ben. Up until the point that I started to hug the porcelain throne, it was a great date.

"Are you just going stare dreamily into space, or are you going to take us out of our misery and fill us in already?" Rae jokes.

"I mean, we've been sitting here all night waiting for you to come home!" Mik practically whines.

I roll my eyes in an attempt to mask my amusement.

"Did he kiss you? Or did you get sick before he had the chance?" Mik asks.

"Oh, he kissed me." I say with a sigh.

The two of them squeal like school girls, and honestly, it's hard to resist the urge to join them. That kiss was amazing, and I'm pretty sure if the waitress on the boat hadn't interrupted us, I may have begun shedding my clothing right there on the deck; cold weather and seasickness be damned. I share all the details about the kiss with the girls, and they hang on my every word, sighing loudly when I finish. As I recount the entire experience, I swear I can feel my lips tingle.

"Wow that sounds amazing. So, swoon worthy." Mikaela says dreamily.

"Yes, up until you started to expel your stomach's contents, it sounds like it was the perfect date." Rae agrees.

"I know, I know." I shake my head at my own mistake. "I should have opened my mouth and told him that boats and I don't mix. But, you guys, I didn't want to come across as high maintenance! Though, in hind sight, I guess that probably would have been better than having him watch me throw my guts up." I say mortified at the memory.

"I actually think it is romantic." Mik gushes.

"Come again?"

"Well, he took care of you Jillybean. He didn't leave you to your own devices. I'm not even sure if I could have stayed with you to watch you hurl."

I already know this, but hearing her say it out loud makes it even more real to me; Benjamin Sapphire is pretty special. And even though I've agreed to go on another date with him, I wasn't completely sure if I could actually go through with it. Between the mortifying evening and my reservations about dating, I was seriously considering he might be better off without me, and just cancel the date. But after what I just shared with the girls, and realizing how great Ben was tonight, I promise myself that I will give our next date a real shot...

BREAKING BENJAMIN

CHAPTER SIX

I've learned, after drilling Mik and Raeva, that Jill loves a good steak, and French fries, and asparagus with hollandaise sauce. So, that's what I've prepped for our dinner tonight. I've got the steak marinating, sides prepped, and a bottle of red already open to breathe. She's supposed to be here at seven, and knowing from our past meetings that she's always prompt, I expect she'll be arriving any minute.

While I don't live in a penthouse, I do live in a very nice loft that I had renovated after I bought the building for the gym, which is located downstairs. It's a large, open space that contains a restaurant-worthy industrial kitchen, a living space filled with a couple of couches, a large flat-screen television, and a bedroom in the back corner of the space that I had sectioned off with some retro glass bricking. I've got rugs scattered throughout on the hardwood floors, and retractable blinds cover the very large warehouse windows that surround three of the outside walls.

I lit some candles, actually ran a vacuum over the floors, and made sure my bed had fresh sheets on it. I wasn't sure what direction our date was going to take, but I certainly hoped that it might end up in the bedroom. I'm dressed comfortably, in a pair of worn jeans and a black t-shirt. Now, all I need is my date. No sooner than that thought crosses through my mind, the bell to the elevator dings.

The speed of my heart ratchets up a few notches as I make my way over to the call button. I press it and speak. "Come on up." I press another button that unlocks the elevator down below and hear the large doors clank shut and then some light rattling of the wires as it begins to rise.

My bare feet pace back and forth a few short steps, and then stop when the doors slide open revealing who I've come to believe is the most beautiful woman in the world. She seems to have followed suit with my casual attire, because she's also wearing a pair of jeans; although, hers are much darker and fit tightly over her long legs. She's got some kind of light cotton top on that's sitting off her shoulders, in a pretty teal color, and has a jacket over her arm.

She holds up a bottle of red wine and beams brightly. "I brought wine!"

I stroll toward her, take the bottle, and using my free hand, wrap it around her waist. I pull her just close enough to place a soft kiss against her cheek. "All I need is you."

She flushes a light pink and lets out a soft sigh as a small smile plays on her lips. "Hi, Ben."

"Hi." I release her and wave my hand over the space in front of us. "Welcome. Not a single wave in sight."

She chuckles and runs a hand down her face to hide her embarrassment. "Ugh. Let's forget about that disaster. Please!"

"Done." I take her hand in mine and start toward the kitchen.

"You look beautiful, by the way."

"I feel like I should take my heels off so we're on even ground." She giggles beside me.

"Angel, we ain't ever gonna be on even ground. You're always going to be floating in a space much higher than me." I turn and slide my gaze down her body. "No matter what you're wearing."

She tucks her chin in as she tries to hide the blush coloring her cheeks. "Ben, you have to stop saying things like that to me."

We reach the kitchen, so I place the bottle of wine on the island and turn, yanking her up against me by our joined hands, a small gasp of surprise coming from her as our bodies crash together. I place my hand under her chin and raise it until I'm gazing into her eyes. "I don't know how other men have treated you, but you deserve to be told every day how goddamn beautiful you are. Every time I see you, you take my breath away. I don't know how you do it, but each time I see you, your even more gorgeous than the time before."

Her lips form a small 'o' shape, and her eyes grow wide. "Oh."

"So, if you're going to be with me, get used to hearing it. You're fucking stunning. Like an angel walking on this earth. I'd almost bet you have wings hidden under that shirt if I didn't already see your bare back the night of the opening."

Her fingers, which were clutched around my biceps a moment ago, have started to trail gently down my arms as something in her gaze shifts. I watch as her tongue darts out and swipes across her lips, leaving them wet and shiny and causing my restraint to finally snap. My hands move up the back of her neck, slide around to grasp her face, and then I crash my lips against hers.

It's not the first time I've kissed her, but it's the first time I've had sparks light up under my eyelids as the heat of her breath mixes with mine and our mouths fuse together. She groans, and I take advantage, sliding my tongue against hers, deepening our kiss. Her fingernails are digging into my arms where she's now clutching them again, her body pressing more tightly against mine. I know she's discovered the growing bulge below my waist when she rubs her core up and down my length, another small moan vibrating against my mouth.

I move my hands to clutch under her ass and lift, urging her to wrap her legs around me, and begin walking blindly toward my bedroom. Her hands are gripping my hair as she tries to control the heat of our kiss, her lips breaking away from me as they begin to nip down my neck. My head falls back, a low growl rolling from my mouth as she latches on and sucks hard for just a second before releasing and moving lower.

My fingers dig into her ass as I yank her tighter against my now fully erect cock, her mouth leaving my neck as her head raises, her gaze locking onto mine, eyes wide in shock. My knees hit the bed at the same time, and I lower her back onto the bed, my body hovering just inches above hers.

"Are we really doing this?" Her question comes out breathy.

I can't believe I'm lying here, on my back, in his bed, and it's only our second date. And it's not because I don't want to be here, I do. So badly. He runs his nose along my neck and across my cheek before he plunges his mouth on mine once more. Our tongues dance furiously with each other, stirring the flame of our desire higher. He pulls back and captures my gaze with his. "Is it too soon?" he pants out in response to my question.

His genuine concern for me, and the fact that he seems to actually be asking for my permission instead of talking me into something I might not want, makes the decision easy for me. I shake my head. "If it is, I don't care," I reply honestly.

Ben reacts by grinding his enormous length against my core, and I nearly combust on the spot. Our mouths fuse together once more, more frantic than moments ago when I would have sworn we could not feel more heat.

Both of us are wearing too many clothes right now, so I slide my hands down his back until I find the hem of his shirt, grasp it in my fingers and start pulling it up to take it off. When he realizes, his lips break away from mine long enough to assist me with the process before slamming back home. My nails dig deep into his back as I grind up against him, needing him urgently.

Ben shifts away from me and yanks me in to a sitting position. I watch as his fingers skim down over my breasts until they find the hem of my shirt, which he bunches in his fingers and then lifts it over my head. I automatically raise my arms as he does and shiver in delight when he takes my smaller hands in one of his larger ones and pushes me back on the bed.

"Stay right there." He orders, and it's so entirely sexy that even the little rebel on my shoulder nods her head obediently.

I suck my bottom lip between my teeth and bite down, welcoming the sting of it. Ben's eyes slide to my mouth, and growls fiercely as he lowers his mouth onto my shoulder and starts peppers kisses in a line straight to my breasts. His mouth finds my nipple over my bra, which

63

isn't difficult since they are currently hard as rocks, and draws it into his mouth with a sharp pull. My hips jerk up into his, once again rubbing against his swollen center, and I moan loudly. He smirks briefly before moving to the other side, giving my other nipple the same attention.

My bra has a front clasp, and he seems to have no issue snapping it open. His large hands slide the fabric off and grasp onto each breast, and I nearly scream out when he squeezes. I can't help the moan that falls from my lips; it's loud and needy. I want his mouth back on my breasts, and I have no trouble letting him know. I grab his hair in both hands and force him back in their direction. He chuckles but obliges none the less. His tongue circles around my nipple before he sucks on it, hard. My body jumps about a mile above the bed. "Oh my God. Yes, Ben!"

He moves to the other breast, eliciting the same response, before finally making his way down, lower, where I am literally aching for him. I am positively throbbing between my thighs. His mouth finds the button of my jeans, and I almost come when the man rips them open with his teeth! *Holy fuck, that is hot.*

He grips the waistband of the denim fabric and slides it off me with remarkable skill. In my dazed state, it takes me a moment to realize that my panties are coming down as well. I have no objections, and in compliance, lift my hips, making the process easier and faster. As my need for him grows to epic proportions, my patience dwindles at the same rate. In an effort to assist him in ridding me of my jeans and panties, I push at the back of my heels with my toes to release my shoes. They fall onto the floor with a loud thud, and then I am completely naked, entirely exposed to him. Both physically and emotionally.

Every wall has come down, and I want to join my body with his more than I want to take my next breath. He leans back over me, but he is still entirely too dressed, and I want him naked. "Uh-uh. I want yours off, too."

My hands move to his top button and tug it free. My eyes flicker to his, and I think I see him hesitate for just a moment before he tugs at the zipper and pushes his jeans down off his legs. When he is fully naked, I swallow hard. I felt him grind up against me before, and I knew he was... large, but Jesus, his cock is huge! He's going to destroy my pussy. I relish the idea. My eyes flicker a little lower, and I remember the prosthetic now that I have my eyes on it. I get it now; the slight hesitation.

"Do you need to take it off?" I ask as I nod my head downwards.

It's the first time I've seen his confidence stutter, his cheeks flushing just the slightest pink. "Do you mind? It's actually easier if I do, and more comfortable."

Shit, all I want is for him to screw my brains out. I catch his gaze and make sure he can see the look in my eyes when I tell him, "Ben, just do whatever you need to do to fuck me already."

His face lights up at my blunt reply, and he shakes his head slightly, as if he cannot believe the words that have just fallen from my lips. He sits up and pulls the prosthetic off with lightning speed, and before I can even blink, he's on top of me, caging me with an arm on either side. I take advantage of this position and allow my hands to explore that magnificent painted chest of his, gliding my fingers over the perfection above me. But hunger soon overtakes me. I need his mouth on mine. I have never been known for my patience, and I am not about to start now. I pull him down until his lips crash onto mine.

His swollen head is sliding against the throbbing between my thighs that is soaking with need. I move my hips up and down to show him just how ready I am for him. He reaches over to the bedside table and pulls out a condom, rolling onto his side to slide it on. He is taking too long; I don't want to wait another second, so I push him onto his back and straddle him. He looks up at me with wide eyes, his lips curled up in surprise. I lower my pussy against his length and slide it up and down, the pressure against my clit pure heaven.

He says something, but I am too lost in my nirvana to even comprehend words. I'm done waiting and move to position myself over him before sliding myself down onto him in one push. I welcome the sting, screaming out my relief as his impressive length impales me. "Yes!"

I rise up until he's almost out of me and slide down again, adjusting to his magnificent cock more quickly this time. Ben thrusts up at the same time and leaves me feeling so impossibly full that I think that he's going to split me in two. We move in perfect sync, as if this was rehearsed a million times and we are competing for finals. I fall into ecstasy as the muscles in my wall begin to tighten around his cock.

Tingles run across every inch of my skin, and I close my eyes as my orgasm begins to crest. I rock myself harder against Ben and sigh as I pulse around him in such welcome relief. Just when I think it's over, he rolls me onto my back and starts to pump into me even more deeply than before. I wrap my legs around him, locking him against me, and meet each of his thrusts with a loud pant. His arms tighten around me as I crest yet again, a second orgasm exploding from me as I scream his name out again, and feel him thrust hard one more time as his yells out his release with me.

We both lay panting for a moment before he rolls over, his semierect cock sliding out of me as he does, and then pulls me close. He wraps his arms around me and kisses the top of my head. "That was fucking amazing," he says, out of breath.

"Yeah, it wasn't too bad," I say, like the smart ass I am.

He lifts his head to look down at me. "Not too bad?"

I shrug against him. "Well, I usually at least get dinner when I'm on a date." My face breaks into a smile as I trace my fingers lazily over his chest.

"Oh, honey, this date is just getting started. I'm going to make you dinner, and then we're going to do this all over again. But better."

"It gets better?"

"For someone who just said it wasn't too bad, I think I'm going to have to do whatever I can to make sure it gets better."

I rise up, look him in the eye, and give him my most devilish smile. "Oh, I'm so up for this challenge Ben."

CHAPTER SEVEN

I've slept with my fair share of women over the years. But fuck me, I don't think I've ever felt this satisfied. Ever. I didn't even scratch the surface with what I want to do to this woman. This was hard and fast and full of fucking heat, but I still need to explore every inch of Jill's delicious body. I want to do it right now, in fact, but my date has requested I feed her, so feed her I will... more than my cock. I chuckle at my own internal thought and shift my gaze as her fingers stop trailing over my stomach and lay flat as she pushes to lean up and look at me.

"What's so funny?" One brow is raised over her gorgeous gray eyes.

The side of my mouth rises in a cocky grin before I lean forward and press my lips against hers. "Just wondering how I got lucky enough to get your gorgeous ass in my bed."

"Trying to distract me with compliments?" She grins back down at me.

"Oh, if I was going to distract you, I would do something like this."

Before she can react, I roll her over and capture her lips in mine, slide a hand over her breast, and gently roll her taut nipple between my fingers. Her mouth opens as a soft moan falls from her lips, and I sweep my tongue inside, loving the feeling of her breath against mine. I kiss her for only a minute, making sure to leave her wanting, and then pull slowly away. "Didn't you say something about me feeding you?"

Her hands snake up and latch onto the longer locks of my hair as she pulls my face close to hers. "I've said it once, Benjamin Sapphire, but I'll say it again. You, sir, are a tease."

I grin salaciously. "Me?"

"Yes. You." She draws my face forward until it's only a hair's breadth from hers and then darts her tongue out, sliding it across my lips in one slow motion. I inhale deeply and force myself to keep my head still instead of crashing my lips onto hers like I desire. "Just don't forget that two can play at that game."

"I like when you're feisty." I snake my own tongue out and trace it over my lips, following the same path hers did. "But you're right. Let's eat first. I want to make sure you have enough energy for what I'm planning to do to you later."

Her eyes widen, and I feel her body shift under me as her cheeks flush a stunning shade of pink. "I think I can live with that plan."

I lower myself the tiny fraction required and place a soft kiss on her lips before pushing myself up and off her. Her eyes roam down my chest so I look down in question and then back at her. "Too much?" I have a lot of ink. I don't see a single mark on her body.

She shakes her head. "No." Her fingers reach out and graze over the wings of the phoenix on my shoulder. "I want to trace every single line with my tongue. It's incredibly sexy." Her eyes shift to meet mine.

"You're incredibly sexy."

My fucking heart skips a beat, then another, and then another. I want to throw her back on this bed right now, shove my cock into her, and claim her as mine. Instead, I muster every ounce of will power I have and push my animalistic needs away for the moment. "You just may be the most perfect woman I've ever met, Jill Baldwin."

Her eyes grow wide for just a second before she blushes and shifts her gaze to her lap. I honestly don't think she's used to receiving compliments, which staggers me because she is truly the most gorgeous and humble woman I can ever remember meeting. Not wanting to embarrass her further, I shift to the end of the bed and move to place my prosthetic back on. I look over my shoulder as I do and address her. "Ready for some dinner? I'm going to make you the best steak you've ever had."

Her face lights up as she smiles and then hops out of the bed. "Yes! I'm starving." She wiggles her eyebrows and smiles even brighter. "Plus, word on the street is that I'm going to need some extra fortitude for the rest of the evening."

She reaches down, plucks the t-shirt I had on earlier off the floor, and pulls it over her head. I watch as she then pulls her panties out of her strewn jeans and slides them up her legs. Did I say she couldn't get any more beautiful? *Fuck me. I was wrong.* Seeing her in my shirt may be the hottest goddamn thing I've ever seen in my life. I rise off the bed, walk over, and pull her into my arms to mumble into her soft waves, "Where in the hell have you been hiding?"

Her arms tighten around me in response, clinging to me for a full minute before she loosens her grip to pull away, her eyes meeting mine with a smile. "I guess good things are worth waiting for."

After I pull on a pair of shorts, and no shirt per her request, we head to the kitchen and work together to cook dinner. I'm pleasantly surprised to learn she's an amazingly good cook and actually gives me some tips on how to grill the asparagus, rather than steam it, for optimal flavor. As soon as I sink my teeth into the tender green stalks and the smoky flavor bursts in my mouth, I moan. Out loud. It's that good. Not a single drop of the hollandaise is needed, not that it stops her from dipping every bite in the yummy sauce. I love that this woman eats with gusto. She wanted her steak rare and her fries crunchy, and I smile as she devours every morsel without apology. Seriously, this woman just keeps getting better and better.

Even though I made promises to have her for dessert, after cleaning up the dinner dishes, we wander over to the big couches in the middle of my living space and fold into one with full glasses of the wine I opened early, continuing the easy conversation that's been flowing between us. She curls her legs underneath her like a cat, her long bare limbs exposed past her thighs where my t-shirt sits.

"So, tell me all the things about you I don't know yet, Ben." Her lips kiss the edge of her glass as she takes a sip of the dark red liquid, her eyes locked on me.

"Tell me what you know and I'll fill in the blanks," I counter, not smugly but challengingly.

She tilts her head in acceptance. "Well, I know you're a Sapphire, which basically means you're rich."

I shrug my shoulders. It's not something I can deny. I was lucky enough to be born to a father who worked his ass off to build this empire. Now, Drew and I run it, and we're able to enjoy and reap the benefits of its success. "Does it bother you that I'm rich?"

She shakes her head back and forth and speaks softly. "No,

because you don't act like you are. You could choose to do whatever you like, live wherever you want with your money, but instead, you live in a loft. You joined the Army. And look what you've done downstairs. I mean, could you be any more selfless?"

I look down into my glass and think about how to respond to this, because I think, initially, when I started the gym, it was purely for selfish reasons, but I decide to just be honest and share this with her. "I'm not quite the savior you paint me to be, Jill. When I lost my leg, I went to a really dark place. I almost got lost there and may not have made it back if it wasn't for my stubborn brother and another really stubborn physical therapist at the hospital."

She shifts closer to me and, completely astonishing me, places her hand on the seam where my prosthetic meets my scarred leg. "This happened in the war?"

I'm not lying when I tell you that not a single person, outside of medical staff, has ever touched my wound. Her touch shifts something inside of me, making me aware of how unbelievably special this woman is. Emotion threatens to steal my voice, so I clear my throat as I try to shake it away, replying softly, "Yes. Our truck hit an IED." I stop and look at her to clarify in case she doesn't understand. "An explosive buried in the ground." She nods, so I continue before I lose my nerve. "It was bad. Really bad. When I woke up, I just remember seeing blood everywhere, and body parts, and feeling terrified when I looked down and saw how mangled my leg was. But it was nothing compared to looking beside me and seeing one of my best friends dead."

I stop then because the old anger of being the one to survive, and my friends not surviving, is boiling under the surface. She doesn't need to see that. And, again, I'm astonished when she moves even closer and takes my hand in hers, squeezing gently. "I'm so, so sorry for your losses, Ben. I can't begin to comprehend what you must have suffered, but I'm really glad your stubborn brother saw you through."

Blinking rapidly to damn the emotion that's trying to break free behind my lids, I shake my head again in wonder. I clear my throat again and continue my story. "So, you see, I needed to do something with all that anger. Once I could stand on my own again," I release her hand for only a moment to knock on my leg to expand on my statement, and then take it back in mine, "I found a way to release some of it and began boxing. When I left the hospital, I wanted a space more private where I didn't feel like everyone was looking at my leg, or if I lost my balance and fell, I didn't have people feeling sorry for me. I bought this building and initially just put a punching bag in. Then I invited some of my brothers, and then they invited some more, and the next thing I knew, I had a full-fledged gym. It would have been selfish of me not to open the doors to other men like me who needed a place to go and didn't have it." I shrug nonchalantly and look up to find her staring at me intently.

She finally graces me with a smile as she moves her head back and forth in a slow motion. "Do you understand how amazing what you've done is? I'm in awe of you, Benjamin. Complete awe."

I look into my glass and then take a sip of wine before replying. I'm embarrassed. I did this for me, and being able to help my other brothers-in-need just happened naturally, not because of anything I did consciously. "Don't be. Be in awe of the men and women who are still out there fighting for us and protecting us. And for the families here waiting with baited breath for them to come home. They are the ones to admire. Not me."

She scoots even closer to me, and I wonder if she's going to climb into my lap, but instead, she grasps my chin between her tiny fingers and pulls my face to look at her. "And that is what makes what you've done so amazing. You take no credit for how much you help these people and feel less for doing it. That makes you one of the most giving men, and maybe, I'm now proud to say, one of the most admired men I have ever had the honor of knowing."

I'm stunned by her words and at a loss as to how to respond to them, so I lean forward and press my lips to hers. Her hand moves from my chin and slides around my neck to deepen the kiss, but it doesn't take a passionate turn. This kiss is different; it's filled with feelings I've never experienced and leaves me breathless with its meaning. Before I can think about it further, she pulls back, places a kiss to my nose, and then slides down and curls into my body.

"Okay, so we've got rich, one-legged, selfless, and amazing kisser out of the way. What else should I know about you, Ben?"

I laugh out loud and pull her closer to me as I do, enjoying the feeling of her warm body pressed in against mine. I tell her about my sister that died in a car accident at sixteen, how hard it was for my family, how much my brother Drew, although younger, has really always taken care of me. I tell her how we spent our summers in Northern California on the beach, surfing, playing football, and chasing girls. I tell her how much I love Hannah and the children she's brought into our lives and how they brought my parents back to life.

We talk for hours, her also sharing her story with me, until we finally grow quiet and just sit in each other's company. Sometime during the night, or early hours of the morning, we both drift to sleep on the couch, her safely encased in my arms. As her soft breaths whisper against my bare chest, my heart is fuller than it's ever felt before.

My eyes flutter open as little rays of sunshine dance across my face. Ben's arm is draped over me, and I can hear the steady beat of his heart. A warmth spreads through me and my lips curl into a smile. I squeeze my eyes shut again, trying to keep reality at bay for just a little longer. I inhale his scent, a faint trace of his cologne mixed with my perfume. The scents complement each other perfectly. I focus on his breathing, and everything inside of me just wants to sneak a peek at him while he's sleeping.

I carefully slip out from the warmth of his arms and momentarily regret it. I park my backside on top of the coffee table and just stare at him. The cold surface under my barely covered ass bothers me at first, but that is forgotten as soon as I lay my eyes on him. He's sleeping peacefully and smiling contently while doing so.

What in the actual fuck? What is happening to me? Who the hell do I think I am, Edward from Twilight staring at people in their sleep? Mega creepy. But fuck me if I don't see the attraction now that I am the one doing it. I stare at him a little while longer, watching his gorgeous chest rise and fall. As I study his tattoos, I resist the urge to touch them, to trace them with my fingers. I feel my heart rate accelerate, and the butterflies are back. *There they are again.* I tell myself. I silently chuckle as my inward voice is singing those words with me. I blink.

"No," I whisper.

My eyes widen when realization hits me. I am falling for him—hard. *I am fucking falling for Benjamin Sapphire.* Suddenly, the butterflies make way for feelings of doom. Panic seizes around my throat. The little nagging voice in the back of my head tells me that a man like Ben doesn't stick around for the long run, and here I am stupid enough to let myself fall for him.

He makes a little growling noise, and it startles me. He turns over, and I release the little breath I didn't know I was holding. I have to get out of here. I am wearing Ben's shirt, and I know I am going to need a little more than that to get home, so I stealthily get up and tiptoe to his bedroom. I gather my clothing, which is scattered all across the room, and shrug into my jeans. I pull Ben's shirt off, which still smells of him. I can't stop myself from bringing it to my nose a final time to inhale his scent before placing it on his bed. With my own top back on, I find my heels at the foot of the bed.

But I don't put them on yet. I don't want the clicking of my heels to wake Ben. I go in search of my jacket, knowing that my cell phone is in the pocket. I don't have to look far; it's hanging on a rack close to the entrance. I press the elevator button and am relieved when the doors slide open. When I step into the elevator, I press the button to go to the lobby and slip my heels on my feet, my heart beating in my throat.

I'm grateful I didn't wake him. I cannot bear the thought of an awkward goodbye. He got me in his bed, like he wanted, and now it's done. And that's okay. Ugh, that's a lie. It meant so much more to me, but I need to cut this off before I get in too deep. If I am falling for this man already, after just a couple dates. Who's to say what I'd feel like in a few weeks? I'm not sure if I'd survive it.

"I've made the right decision," I tell myself as the doors slide open.

When I get out of the cab, Rae is standing at the curb with some cash in her hand. Mikaela is pacing behind her. I didn't take my purse to Ben's last night, and I had no money for the cab I hailed. Tears burn behind my eyelids when I see my two besties. I sent out a 911 text on my way back and here they are. No questions asked, they are just here.

Raeva hands the cabby the cash and tells him to keep the change. She turns toward me and must see the look on my face because she immediately pulls me into an embrace. That's when the dam breaks. In the middle of the street, in the brisk New York City morning air. While hordes of people buzz around us.

"Awe, honey. Shhhh," she says as she ushers me into our building.

Mikaela has walked ahead of us and called for the elevator. We walk into it, and when the doors slide to a close, I realize that for the first time since I moved in to the building, I didn't even greet the doorman. I'm not sure why I am focusing on that right now. We ride up to the penthouse, but nobody says a word. The elevator is filled with echoes of my not so silent sobbing.

I'm not sure why I am crying like this; I feel ridiculous. After all, I am the one who snuck out of Ben's place. I am the one who allowed myself to start falling for him, and I am the one who fell into bed with him. The elevator door opens, and we step into the hallway just as Mika is stepping out of their penthouse. I use my sleeve as a makeshift hanky and wipe my eyes. When his gaze lands on me, his brow shoots up and his eyes flicker from his wife to his sister before landing back on me again.

"Is everything okay?" he asks.

Raeva stalks toward him and gets on her tiptoes to plant a kiss on his lips. "Yes, baby. Just girl stuff."

He looks at me and gives me a half-smile and a nod. "Okay then, I'll guess I will let you ladies get to it then."

Mika kisses his wife and walks over to kiss his sister's cheek. Then he stops in front of me and places his hand on my shoulder. "I'm not sure what is going on, but whatever you need, I'm here." Then he leans in and kisses my cheek as well.

I smile weakly at him as I thank him, but I am genuinely grateful, because I know he means it. With that, Mika turns and steps into the elevator, and we turn and step into our penthouse. We head straight for the living area where I curl up onto the couch, and the girls follow suit.

"So, Jillybean, are you going to tell us what happened?" Rae asks. I nod.

"Did he hurt you?" Mik asks.

"No."

My two friends share a look.

"You had sex and it was terrible?" Raeva says as she wrinkles her nose.

"Oh, God no. I mean, we had sex. In fact, the best sex of my life is more accurate."

She looks at me skeptically.

"I swear. Ben is great. Last night was amazing."

The two of them look at me confused.

"So, I'm not sure what the problem is," Mikaela says.

I sigh. "I like him."

Mikaela frowns, but Raeva's expression shows me that she gets it.

"You like him and you're running," she says, matter of factly.

I nod once more. "But it's not as simple as that, guys. I am a realist. This thing was never going to work out. Sure, Ben likes me just fine. But I am not the kind of woman that a Sapphire wants to settle down with, and I can't allow myself to let this get any further."

Raeva shakes her head. "Jillybean, I flove you. You know that. But I wouldn't be a good bestie if I didn't tell you this; you realize that you are your own worst enemy, right?"

"Being realistic is being my own worst enemy?" I snap back.

She chuckles. "Defensive much? You know you only get like that when you know for a fact that you are wrong. Just saying," she retorts smugly.

I roll my eyes, but even I know that the irritation I feel toward her right now is misdirected. The person I am really angry at is myself. The thing is, I'm not sure if I am annoyed because I let myself catch feelings, or that I ran from them like a coward.

"Listen, you can still change your mind. You snuck out? He doesn't need to know you did. We can always tell him that you had an early meeting and didn't want to wake him?"

I shake my head. "No, I can't see him again."

"Jilly—"

"No, I mean it," I interrupt sternly.

They both hold up their hands.

I sigh again. "Listen, I know it's hard for you guys to understand, but I am doing this to protect myself. I just can't risk him breaking my heart. I know he doesn't intend to, but that is where this will end—in heart break. And I need to break things off before it gets too hard to do so. Besides, I am doing business with them. I should have never mixed business with pleasure."

My besties share another look, and I know that they are skeptical. But, never the less, they pull me into a group hug.

"If that's what you want, we support you," Mik tells me.

There is a knock on the front door, and the three of us look at each other. There is another knock, and we all just look at the door for a moment before, finally, Mikaela rises to her feet and goes to answer.

Rae and I duck down on the couch and peek over it as she opens the door. We both chuckle when we see it's just Mark, one of Mikaela's assigned security guys. He hands her an enormous bouquet of white lilies, and I already know who they are for and whom they are from. My stomach knots up as Mik approaches me. She places the flowers on the coffee table and plucks out the card. She holds it out for me, but I shake my head. I can't bring myself to read it because I know that the words on there will be perfect and that my resolve will weaken the moment I read them.

"Are you sure?" she asks.

I swallow hard, press my lips tightly together, and nod my head.

"Do you want to keep the flowers?"

I can't look at them without feeling an ache in my chest, so I shake my head. She nods thoughtfully, proceeds to pick up the flowers, and walks toward the kitchen.

Rae scoots closer to me and wraps her arm around me. She pulls me closer and hugs me from the side. "Honey, I can't say that I understand your reasoning, or even that I agree with it. But I support whatever it is that you want, okay?"

I lay my head on her shoulder and nod.

CHAPTER EIGHT

It's been three days since I woke on my couch to find my arms empty and Jill gone. Three days of unanswered texts and phone calls to her. Three days that I've sent bouquets of her favorite flowers to both her office and her penthouse. Two days of calls to Mikaela, demanding she tell me what's wrong with Jill, and still no answers, only evasion. Mikaela says she's extremely busy working and hasn't seen her to even speak with her. Fucking girl code. I know without a doubt Mikaela's covering for her.

What I don't understand is what the hell happened between her falling asleep in my arms and her disappearing from thin air the next morning. What the hell happened that she won't answer any of my calls or texts? The night we spent together was one of the best of my life. I have never felt a connection or as open with another woman as I do with her. There is no way I am letting her run away from me now.

I punch the bag in front of me one more time for good measure and then lean my exhausted body against it in defeat. I've been punching the shit out of it for the last two hours, and my knuckles are red and swollen. I'm surprised they haven't bled out under the tape yet. I'm going crazy waiting for some kind of message from her and at my wit's end over what I should do next. Letting out a deep breath, I push myself off the bag and head toward the shower.

After rinsing off two hours of sweat in steaming hot water, I change into a pair of jeans and a hoodie. I decide to go see the one person who might understand more than anyone what it's like when the woman you crave just disappears.

Leaving the building, I walk outside into the crisp fall air. It's days like this that I wish I could still ride my bike. I've talked to some guys that have had their bikes modified to allow them to be able to ride again, but I just haven't gotten that far yet. Instead, I walk into the alley beside my building and slide into my Dodge Charger. It's a badass car and makes up for the fact that I can't swing my leg over a bike on afternoons like this.

I put the key in the ignition and turn it, the engine roaring to life, and for good measure, I press on the gas, revving it loudly before I shift into reverse and out into traffic. I'm in front of our hotel on Park Avenue in twenty minutes and hand the keys to the valet driver who greets me by name as I exit the vehicle. "Keep it close. I won't be long."

"Yes, sir." He doesn't give me a tag. He knows who I am. Being a Sapphire definitely has its perks. I stroll through the lobby of the hotel to the elevator and press the floor number for his office. The elevator glides to its destination in seconds, and the doors swish open for me to exit. I stride down the hallway and smile at Felicia, sitting at her desk outside the large dual-office doors of my destination.

"Mr. Sapphire!" She smiles and exclaims in surprise. "Is the other Mr. Sapphire expecting you?"

I stop short of her desk and grimace. "Felicia, please, for the hundredth time, just call me Ben."

"Oh no! I could never do that, Mr. Sapphire." She shakes her head so hard you would think I just asked her to crawl across the floor on her hands and knees and lick the dirt off my boots.

"Really, you can. Actually, I insist." I watch as her eyes pop wide in shock at my order. "Just call me Ben. Mr. Sapphire is my father and makes me feel old."

"Okay, um, Ben." Her face turns an extremely dark shade of pink as she says my name, and I can't help the smile that forms on my lips. It's the first smile it's formed in days. "The other Mr. Sapphire," she lowers her voice to a whisper, "Drew," she continues uncomfortably, pointing to his office doors, "he's in. He's alone, so you can just go on in."

It's strange, but I just want to give her a hug to let her know that her protection of my brother, and her need to show us so much respect, doesn't go unnoticed and is appreciated. But, of course, I don't. I can only imagine what color she would turn then. Instead, I gently pat her hand as I thank her and then move past to knock on the door.

I don't bother waiting for an answer before I enter. Drew's attention shifts from his computer, a look of surprise and then subtle annoyance crossing his face as it lands on mine. "Ah, I should have known. Only you enter unannounced, Benny Boy." He leans back in his chair and shakes his head lightly, steepling his fingers in front of him as he does. "I was wondering when you'd show up."

I cock my head as I plop myself into one of the leather chairs in front of his desk. "Why's that?"

"Jill Baldwin's disappearing act?" he counters smugly.

"How the fuck do you know about that? I haven't talked to you in almost a week." I sit up straighter in the chair, anxious to see what information he has.

"Oh, I'm not supposed to know a thing." His brows raise as he shakes his head. "And, believe me, I wish I didn't. But those women had a little hen session the other day, and it's all I've heard Hannah talk about since."

I widen my eyes and wave my hands in exasperation. "Well, what the fuck is going on?"

"Apparently, Jill had some kind of melt down about how she may or may not be feeling about you and has gone into retreat mode." He shrugs his shoulders.

"What the fuck does that mean? Retreat mode?" I question hotly.

"Jesus, I don't know, Ben." He runs his fingers through his hair and then lets out a long sigh. "She's been burned pretty badly in the past by a couple of men. Not just one, from what Hannah says. I think she's cagey about trusting or caring for anyone again."

I shake my head in frustration. "Drew, I've been nothing but a perfect gentleman to this woman. Done everything I can to assure her I'm on the level here. I mean, I shared shit with her that I've never shared with anyone. Not even you."

I flinch as I see an expression of hurt slide over his face and then just as quickly disappear, and groan inwardly that I've offended him. I continue in an effort to try to explain my way back into his good graces. "It's just different with her. Even though we haven't spent a lot of time together, I feel like my soul has known her forever. She's awakened something in me."

"Look, I get it, Ben. I was there with Hannah." He chuckles as his eyes roll back in memory. "And you know how hard it was for me to get her to see me and believe she wasn't wrong for doing so."

"So, what the hell am I supposed to do now? Not see her? Sit around and wait? Not being able to talk to her and fix this is driving me crazy." I stand and walk to the large window behind my brother and stare down at the park entrance below.

"Go find her, man." He rises and comes to stand next to me. "Funny story." He points to a bench sitting just to the left of the entrance. "When I thought I had completely lost Hannah, I found her sitting in the pouring rain, right there. My destiny was sitting right outside, and all I had to do was go down and make her mine."

I look over at him, my brows creased. "What the fuck is your point, Drew?"

He rolls his eyes and slaps a hand on my shoulder. "You don't have to wait for her to show up, Benny. You know where to find her. Go get her."

"Yeah? Just like that? Go invade her space?"

"Yeah. Just like that." His hand grips around my arm and shoves me in the direction of the door. "What the hell are you waiting for? You've got nothing to lose, right?"

I tilt my head, shrug my shoulders, and meet my brother's challenging look. "If this makes things worse, I'm gonna come back here and kick your ass, little brother."

"You can come and give it your best shot. Now, get the hell out of here." He scoffs and points to the door.

Ten minutes later, I'm back in my car and headed to Serenity. My gut tells me that's where I'll find her. She's completely invested in her company, and I'm guessing she's buried herself in work. I'm not sure what I'm going to say when I see her, but I pray, when she does come face to face with me, she'll tell me what the fuck is wrong.

Another fifteen minutes later, I pull into a parking garage a block down from the spa and then quickly walk the distance to its entrance. It's after four, and the waiting room is empty and quiet. I'm assuming they are probably done taking appointments today, and most likely are in the process of finishing up whatever clients may still be in-house. No one's at the front desk, so I take a seat in the lobby and wait for someone to appear.

I pick up a magazine on the table and begin absently flipping through the pages when I hear voices around the corner. I go on high alert and stand, tip-toeing a bit closer when I hear Jill's name being spoken in the conversation.

"Yes, that guy, the tattooed one with the missing leg!"

They both giggle and shush each other at the same time.

"Well, from what I heard, what he's missing from one leg, he makes up with another. If you know what I mean!" Another round of giggles ensues, and I roll my eyes at their immaturity. Really, they're gossiping about my dick? My irritation comes to a screeching halt when I hear Jill's name again.

"Anyway, I heard Jill tell Maria that if he comes in here again that she wants nothing to do with him. Maria can handle any and all business with him."

"But why? One leg or not, the guy is smoking hot."

"Something about having had enough damaged goods in her life and doesn't need anymore."

My heart lurches in my chest, and the blood in my veins turns icy cold as it runs through my body, every inch of my skin hardening at what I just heard. *She thinks I'm damaged goods?* I shake my head in disbelief. She seemed totally fine with me, and my leg, the other night. Was it all an act? I can't stand to listen to another word these women are whispering.

I take a step backward and move to spin around and slam right into a side-table, the potted plant on it smashing to the ground. *Fuck me and my goddamn leg that doesn't feel a thing!* Before I can escape, the gossiping girls appear from around the corner, their expressions changing from wonder to shock as they recognize me. I'm quite sure, based on the looks on both of their faces, they realize I just heard every word they've said.

They both begin apologizing and move to help with the plant, but I place my hand out flat. "Just stop." They comply instantly and freeze. Without another word to them, I spin on my heel and leave the building as quickly as I arrived.

My blood, moments ago cold as ice from the words I overheard between the two women at the spa, is now flowing like lava through my veins as my rage grows. *Damaged fucking goods?* I shake my head in disgust. Not at her, but at myself. For believing that a woman like Jill saw past my disability to see the man that I am. Who the hell was I kidding? Pieces of me are missing. Just call me Broken Benjamin. A woman liked her deserves someone whole.

I reach my car and yank the door open, throwing myself behind the driver's seat. I stare at the concrete wall in front of me and have a sudden urge to start the engine, put the car in reverse, and then plow forward until I smash head-on into its hard surface. Closing my eyes, I shake my head again. I haven't had dark thoughts like these in a very long time. If caring for a woman drives me to thoughts like this, maybe her not wanting me is for the best.

Banging my hands on the steering wheel, I let out a roar of frustration. It doesn't help relieve one bit of the pain that now seems to be clenching my heart. How is it possible after knowing this woman for only a few short weeks that I could feel so thoroughly gutted? I lay my head on the steering wheel in defeat, already knowing the answer to my own question but trying in vain to push it to the recesses of my mind. I need to force her and whatever I was feeling to the very back corner of my heart and forget about her. Forget her smile, the silkiness of her skin under my fingers, her fresh rain scent, the way she felt under me, and especially how it felt when she trailed her fingers over me.

I lift my head and try to shake it clear. Darkness creeps in along the edges of my brain, and I know I need to move before it takes over completely. I start the car and exit the garage, paying the attendant as I do. I drive aimlessly for an hour and then head back to the hotel. Grabbing my cell phone off the passenger seat, I tell Siri to call Drew. Seconds later, his voice sounds on the other end.

"Benny, how'd it go?" He's upbeat and eager to hear my news, but I'm in no mood for small talk.

"Meet me at the bar in ten." I hit end without waiting for a response. I'm sure that alone will tell him what he needs to know.

Traffic is heavier now, so it's another fifteen minutes before I walk in and see him sitting on the far end. He's got a drink in his hand and another waiting on the bar in front of the stool beside him. I slide onto it, grab what I know will be whiskey, and drink it in two long gulps. He doesn't say a thing, just lifts a finger and motions for the bartender to bring another. He does. Quickly. I tell him to leave the bottle. After a nod from my brother, he does and then scurries away.

We sit in silence for a few very long minutes before either one of us says anything. He finally breaks and starts the conversation. "You want to talk about it?"

"Not really." I drain my second glass of whiskey and grab the bottle to pour myself another.

"So, am I just supposed to sit here and watch you get fucked up? Because, really, I've got a few more important things I could be doing right now."

I turn my head and stare at him, my insides turning black with anger. "Can you just sit here with me and be my goddamn brother? If I want to get my feelings out, I'll call a fucking counselor."

He stares right back at me, reaches for the bottle to pour himself another drink, and shifts back on his stool, his gaze never leaving mine. "I'll sit here all damn night if you need me to, Ben, but I can't read your mind."

"She said I'm damaged goods," I spit out and turn my head to break our eye contact, heat flaring in my cheeks.

"What?" His glass slams down on the bar, and I hear liquid slosh out and land on the bar. "She fucking said that to you?"

I swallow my embarrassment and turn my attention back to him. "Not directly."

"Wait, what?" His brow creases as his head cocks to one side.

"I overheard some of her staff talking. They apparently are under orders to make sure I'm kept clear of Ms. Baldwin and mentioned it was because I'm damaged goods." My brows raise matter-of-factly as I finish explaining.

He's speechless for several long minutes before finally blowing out a long breath. "I don't know what to say to that."

"I do." I take a swig from my glass and slam it down. The warm liquid is starting to turn the black edges of my brain to gray and I like it. "Fuck her."

"Don't you think you should talk to her?"

I watch as he uses a napkin to wipe up the whiskey he spilled a moment ago. "What the fuck for? More insults? More fake smiles? No thanks." I shake my head and let more of the warm liquid slide down my throat.

"Ben, you know how gossip is. Shit gets misconstrued, made up, twisted, and honestly, this doesn't sound like the Jill I met. I don't take her for someone to dismiss another over a disability, let alone speak about it to others."

I shrug. I'm tired of talking about this shit. "Whatever. I've been calling her for days. She's obviously made her choice."

"So, now what?"

"What do you mean?" I glance over at him.

"What's your plan? Are we ditching the Serenity deal?"

Ah, I knew business was going to play into this sooner or later. It always does with my type A, controlling as hell brother. I scoff. "My plan is to sit here and get fucked up. Then maybe I'll pick up the first gorgeous woman I see, bring her up to a suite, and fuck Jill out of my system." I grin wickedly at him, pretending that's all I would actually need to forget a woman like Jill, that I even want to be with another woman, and then continue. "You want Serenity still; it's all yours. But I'm out."

"I could give two shits about the deal, Ben. It's not like we need the goddamn money. If you're out, I'm out." He takes a sip of his drink and keeps talking. "But instead of wasting away here, why don't you head out to my place in the Hamptons? It's empty, and its quiet. You can do whatever the hell you need to for a few days."

I cock my head in his direction and consider his suggestion. Getting out of this city, away from my loft that still carries her lingering scent, to stare at the shore for a few days while I shake her out of my system actually seems like a good idea. "Okay."

"Really?" He's surprised and I don't blame him. I'm not usually this agreeable.

"Sure. What the fuck else have I got to do?" I take another drink and then say quietly, "My bed is haunted with her scent. I'm not ready to deal with that yet."

His hand reaches out and clasps around my arm in a tight, knowing grip. "Let me get David to drive you. He's got my car outside and waiting for me anyway. I'll take a cab home."

"Right now?" I question in surprise.

"Bring the damn bottle with you if you need to, Benny. Let's just get you the hell out of here."

I roll over on the couch, my arm smacking into the empty whiskey bottle sitting on the nearby coffee table and it crashes to the floor. I sit up, grabbing my forehead as I do, and listen. Did I just hear the doorbell ring? I stand, my leg stiff as fucking hell from being in the prosthetic all night, and glance out the window. It's pouring and the sky is a dark, turbulent gray, which matches my mood perfectly.

I turn my head abruptly again when I hear loud knocking against the door. Okay, so I'm not crazy. But the who the hell would be crazy enough to come out here in the middle of a fucking raging storm? I stride to the door and yank it open, not bothering to look through the peephole first, and my mouth falls open.

Standing before me, looking like a drowned rat, is a shivering Jill. I stare at her for a long moment, trying to decide if I just want to slam the door in her face, but of course, I can't. No matter how pissed off and hurt I am over what she said, I'm not a fucking asshole, and I'm not going to leave her standing in the freezing rain. I step to the side and motion for her to come in. "What are you doing here, Jill?"

BREAKING BENJAMIN

CHAPTER NINE

Jill – 24 hours earlier

The knock on my office door startles me. Every time there is a knock, I am afraid that Ben will be on the other side of it. Or maybe I am secretly hoping that it's him. "Yes?" I say out loud.

The door opens, and Aisha peeks her head around the corner. "Hey, Jill, you got a minute?"

I smile. "Sure, come in."

Aisha steps into my office, closely followed by Anna. The two of them stand before me as if they are students in front of the principal. I raise a brow. "Did something break?"

They share a look, one that I don't like.

"Okay, what broke?"

"Nothing broke," Anna mutters. "But we did kind of mess up."

I frown. "Sorry, ladies, I am very busy right now, so can you please spit it out?" My voice is laced in irritation I can't hide.

They share yet another look. "We were talking in the hall, and we think—no, we *know* that he heard us."

"What in the world are you talking about?"

Another shared look.

"Will the two of you stop doing that?" I bark.

Anna bites her lip. "We were talking about you and Mr. Sapphire... And, well, we may have been joking a little bit and he overheard us," Aisha says.

My stomach drops.

"I swear, we didn't know he was there," Anna adds.

My nostrils flare involuntarily as I press my lips tightly together. I close my eyes for a moment, pinching the bridge of my nose between my thumb and index finger in an attempt to reign in my temper. "Where is Mr. Sapphire now? And don't you dare share another damn look."

"He left."

"He left?"

"And what exactly was said that upset him so?"

Both of their faces scrunch up, and I already know that I am *not* going to like what I am about to be told. "Well, I was telling Aisha that I overheard you tell Maria that she was to deal with Ben—um, I mean, Mr. Sapphire—and she asked me why. So, I told her that you said you were tired of damaged goods."

Holy fuck. Oh my God. He thinks that I called him damaged goods?

"The fact that you two know better than to talk trash in my place of business is one thing, and I promise you two now that I will not tolerate this if it happens again."

Aisha and Anna nod.

"Not that it is any of your business, but you were grossly mistaken. What I actually told Maria is that Ben is too good to be dealing with damaged goods. *Me* being said damaged goods."

Anna bites her lip, and I see tears glistening in her eyes. "We are really sorry. We promise, we won't ever do anything like this again."

Just imagining how he must have felt when he heard them talk like that makes me sick to my stomach. "See to it that it doesn't. I wasn't kidding. Anything like this again and I will not hesitate to fire you on the spot."

Their eyes widen.

"Understood?"

They nod in unison.

I wave at the door, indicating for them to leave, which they do, fast and with their tails between their legs. I pick up my cell and scroll quickly to his number. It rings and rings and rings. Fuck. No answer. I punch in a text, and seconds later, Raeva responds, informing me that she is on her way with a car.

I try Ben again, but this time it doesn't even ring; it goes straight to voicemail. Ugh. I grab my keys and my purse and head to the front of the building so that I won't waste any more time than I need to. I pace the pavement in front of Serenity, stewing, a mixture of anger and anguish overflowing me in waves. People who pass me give me appraising looks, but I don't even care. A town car pulls over just ten minutes after I texted Raeva, and I recognize it to be one of the Kingsley vehicles. Raeva's driver-slash-security guard, Simon, gets out and opens the door for me. I smile at him and thank him as I slide into the car next to her.

"What is the emergency? Where are we headed?" she asks.

"Ben's place."

She raises her brow but instructs Simon to head to Ben's place.

"Now, what the hell is going on?"

I am still shaking with anger when I tell her everything Aisha and Anna told me.

"Shit," she says when I am done talking.

"I know."

Raeva leans in and instructs Simon to step on it. "Yes, ma'am."

We pull in front of Ben's place just minutes later, and I practically fly out of the car before we have even come to a full stop. "Wait for me, please," I yell over my shoulder.

I run up to the elevator across from the gym and press the button. I wait a beat and press again. Damn it. I pull my cell from my pocket and try to dial his number again, knowing that he won't answer, but still, I try.

I sigh as I slide the phone back into my pocket. I turn around and see that the gym is open. Maybe he's there? I stride over to the gym entrance and walk to the front desk. A pretty redhead is on the phone, giving someone a piece of her mind. My first thought is that *I like this girl*. She's feisty. She smiles and holds up a finger before finishing up the call.

"Hi, my name is Stacy. Welcome to Baker-Landon-Rose Memorial Gym. How can I help you today?" she asks me.

I sheepishly smile at her. "Hi, I'm Jill. I am actually looking for Ben."

She looks me over. "Hmmm, so you're Jill, huh?" she says with a smirk. "I've got to hand it to him; he's got excellent taste."

I feel my cheeks redden, and I'm not sure if it's the compliment, the fact that she clearly has heard about me, or both.

"Oh, and humble, too. Score," she jokes.

I smile shyly at her, not quite knowing what to say.

"I'm sorry, Ben isn't here. He called earlier to say that he was going to be away for a few days. I assumed he was going to be out of town with you."

I'm not sure why that surprises me. But, also, now I am stuck. How am I going to find him? I thank Stacy for her time and make my way back to the car. Simon sees me coming and comes around to open the door. I slide next to Rae feeling defeated. I sigh loudly.

"Not home?" she asks.

"Nope, and not at the gym either. The girl at the front desk told me that he is going to be out of town for a bit."

I drop my head backwards. "What am I going to do now? I can't bear the thought of him thinking that I think of him as anything but amazing."

We drive home in silence, and when we get to the penthouse, I am not in the mood to talk to anyone. I kick off my shoes and crawl into bed, not even bothering to take of my clothes. I wrap myself in the duvet like a little caterpillar in a cocoon. I try to call Ben once more, but it goes straight to voicemail again. So, I punch in a text, asking him to please call me. I sigh and bury my face in the pillow. And I don't emerge till morning...

Loud knocking on my bedroom door has me sitting straight up.

"Wake up, sleepyhead."

I groan. "What do you want, Rae?"

"Open the door, Jillybean. We have a phone call to make."

I walk to the door and flip the lock then practically crawl back to the bed.

"Really? You didn't even bother undressing?" Rae says as she wrinkles her nose.

"Are you here just to lecture me, Mom?" I say a little more

irritated than I intended.

"Testy this morning, are we?"

'I'm sorry, Rae. I'm just feeling like crap. I still have not been able to reach Ben or heard back from him, and I don't know what to do."

"Well, luckily for you, your person is brilliant," she says with a triumphant smirk.

I raise a brow. "That a fact?"

"Yup."

"And what brilliant idea do you have, pray tell?"

"I know how to find Ben..."

She has definitely got my attention now.

"How?" I say eagerly.

"We call Hannah."

Hannah is awesome, even though she makes it abundantly clear how upset she is that Ben is hurt. She listens to my side of the story; me telling her everything because, for some reason, I feel like I owe her the entire truth. We are not particularly close, but I have always liked her. She tells me where to find him and makes me promise to make it better. I promise that I will try. She clearly loves her brother-in-law dearly. I ask Raeva if I can borrow the faster-than-lightening car she received for her birthday so I can make it to Drew and Hannah's place as quickly as possible. She hands me the keys without hesitation, and smiling gratefully, I hug my bestie and thank her.

"Go get your man."

The ride seems to take forever, and of course, it would because it is a pretty long ride. It takes just a little under two hours from Manhattan to the Hamptons, and that is if traffic isn't crazy. But I am impatient to see him. And, let's be honest here, patience isn't one of my strong points. I make good time, though. My mind is racing the entire time. I look ahead and see dark clouds in the distance and idly wonder if it's a bad omen. The GPS tells me that I'm ten minutes out, which pulls me out of my thoughts and back to reality. It's only now that I notice I am bouncing my knee like its doing a jig. I feel restless and rake a hand through my hair. I've been gripping the steering wheel so tightly that my hands actually hurt. And, like the bad omen I was afraid of, the sky opens up and rain starts to pour down as if the heavens are flooding.

Great.

I am grateful when I pull up and see lights on in the house. I park in the driveway and sit in the car for a few minutes, just staring at the front door. Desperately, I try to control my rapid breathing and calm the nerves that have crept up from deep within. I finally get out of the car and brave the pouring rain, trying to minimize the damage. Even though I run as fast as I can, by the time I reach the front door and use the knocker, I am soaked from head to toe.

After pounding a second time and becoming even more drenched, the door finally swings open and I actually flinch in surprise at his disheveled appearance. I realize instantly that no amount of preparation would have helped to control the array of mixed feelings swirling through me at this very moment in time. The hurt in his expression, the unfamiliar flash of anger that mars those always sparkling eyes of his, is almost too much to bear. Especially knowing that I am the one who caused it.

"Hi," I whisper through trembling lips.

He steps aside and motions for me to come in. "What are you doing here, Jill?"

"I had to see you. I had to explain."

"There really is no need. I think I get it."

I sigh. "Ben, you really don't understand. I—"

"I am missing a leg, Jill, but there is not a damn thing wrong with my hearing."

"Damn it, Ben. Will you just shut up for a second and hear me out?"

He raises a brow but gestures for me to continue.

"First, I should have called you back to begin with to thank you for the flowers and to explain my actions. Please believe me when I tell you it had nothing to do with you. This is all me and my fear of letting people in. I swear." I take a step closer to him and fix my gaze on his. "What you heard those two women say, it was them repeating something I said but in the wrong context. Yes, I told Maria to deal with you regarding business because I didn't know if I could remain strong in your presence. When she asked me why, I told her that you've had enough damaged goods in your life, and that you didn't need more. And it's true, Ben. I am broken. You deserve someone so much better than me."

Tears are flowing freely down my face, but I continue through my sobbing. "You may be missing a leg, Ben, but you are whole. I don't give a fuck about your leg. You are more of a man than anyone I have ever encountered. I know that I've screwed up, but I didn't want you thinking that I thought that way about you."

He's silent for a moment and then speaks matter-of-factly. "You shouldn't have driven here in this weather. What were you thinking?"

An exasperated chuckle slips through my tears. "I had to see you. I had to try to explain. The thought of hurting you, I can't accept that. I tried calling, but you wouldn't answer. So, here I am." I shrug my shoulders.

"Yes, speaking of that. How did you find me?"

"Hannah," I admit. "But don't be mad at her. She ripped me a new one before hearing my side."

He seems to relax some, because he smiles for the first time since I arrived. "She can be a giant pain in my backside, but I love her," he tells me with affection in his voice.

Our gazes meet, and we start to move to one another, like magnets. But then, suddenly, he stills. "We need to get you out of those wet clothes. I'm sure Hannah has something you can fit in to, and you can use the shower in the guest room." He motions to the stairway. "It's the second door on the right up there. I'll leave some clothes on the bed for you."

I'm not sure what I was expecting, but I feel a twinge of disappointment. I know I have no right to, since I am the one who ruined any chance of us being together. So, I plaster a smile on my face and thank him before heading to the room he directs me to. I take a quick shower and dry my hair, and when I emerge from the bathroom, I find a pair of jeans and a sweater laying on the bed. Thoughtfully, he also miraculously provided underwear that still has the tags on them. My bra is still soaked so I forgo wearing one. Once I am dressed, I go on the hunt for Ben and find him in the kitchen, making sandwiches.

"Hey there," I say, a bit shyly.

"Hey there, yourself." He smiles gently at me, those dimples I love so much appearing. "I made us some coffee, and I thought I'd feed us."

Ben hands me a plate with a baguette, and I gratefully accept. I didn't realize how hungry I was until I smelled the food. We head to the breakfast nook and sit. I want to tell him that I was wrong, that I've missed him, and that I want us to try to work things out. But before I have a chance to open my mouth, he opens his.

"I'm glad you came to straighten things out."

I smile at him, a glimmer of hope spearing through my heart.

"I had some time to think before you showed up. I realize that perhaps you were correct all along and that we should have kept things strictly professional between us. I want you to know that what happened with you was special to me, but I think it's pretty clear that we are probably better off as friends."

I feel like he has just punched me in the gut. As quickly as my appetite appeared, it disappears. I take a bite anyway, because I am not sure that I can keep my voice from breaking if I speak right now. So, instead, I chew and nod my head.

"If you are still interested, we should push ahead with our deal. I don't want what happened to affect your willingness to work with us."

Forcing a smile, I take another bite and nod. "Thank you," I tell him with the most even tone I can muster up. My heart is broken into a thousand pieces and laying in front of our feet between us. I am not sure how to feel or how to react. All I know is I deserve this, that I was right all along. I knew this would end in heart break, only the culprit wasn't Ben. It was me.

By the time we finish eating, the weather seems to have improved, so I inform him that I need to be headed back to the city. I thank him for hearing me out and offer work as my excuse to leave. He doesn't argue. We hug as we say goodbye, and I inhale his scent one more time before I whisper goodbye and practically stumble to the car and drive away.

CHAPTER TEN

As Jill leaves, I close the door behind her and lean my head against the door jamb, fighting an internal battle about chasing after her or letting her go. For once, reason prevails, but it doesn't stop me from pushing off the frame and moving to the closest window to watch as she slides into the sleek car she arrived in. It's several minutes before I hear the engine come to life, and I wonder if she's feeling as much regret as me. The car pulls out of the long drive, but I still don't look away until I can no longer see the red taillights through the rain.

I hope I didn't just make the biggest fucking mistake of my life. I believe every word that fell from her sad pink lips, and I also know without a shadow of a doubt that she feels as much for me as I do for her. But I also know, especially after feeling the darkness begin to creep into my soul yesterday, that I absolutely can't let that happen again. Opening myself up to her, even just the small fraction I'd allowed so far, made me far more vulnerable than I wanted to be.

I stand at the window, staring at the rain pouring down, until my stump begins to throb in complaint. I've had the damn prosthetic on for way too long and my body has had enough. I tear myself away and decide a visit to the hot tub is in order. Drew was smart enough to build an enclosure around the tub so that it could be used year-round, and I could kiss him right now for his brilliance. No one is here, so I decide to live on the wild side and strip naked instead of finding a suit. I remove my leg when I reach the edge of the tub, sliding my body down into the steaming hot water with a sigh of relief.

As hard as I try not to let my thoughts wander to Jill, it's the only place my mind seems to want to be. I know, even in the short time we spent together, that she could have been the one and it's the first time I'm allowing myself to admit it. Now that she's gone, of course. I chuff out loud as I think of the old cliché, 'you'll know when the right person comes along' and feel pissed that it's actually fucking true. "So, why'd you let her go, asshole?" I say it out loud, even though I know there's no one around to hear it, but maybe to make sure I realize I may have just fucked up royally. I'm a fucking coward for pushing her away instead of putting myself in the line of fire again, but dammit, the thought of any more loss in my life is more than I think I could bear right now. No, I made the right decision. I just need to learn to live with it. I'll find other women to spend my time with; that has never been a problem for me. I blow out a long breath, lean my head back, and force myself to push her out of my conscience.

I've been back in the city for the last two days and know a visit to Drew and Hannah's is overdue, so I find myself leaving my loft and walking one block down to their place. Yeah, it's convenient having them so close, and nice. Knowing I have loving people only a few doorsteps away provides a comfort to me that I truly cherish. I make my way through the lobby and into the elevator, the doorman nodding a friendly greeting at me as I pass. I punch the button for their place, wait until the doors slide back open when the elevator stops, and exit onto their floor.

They own the two top floors of the building. But, I mean, hey, they already have two kids and it wouldn't surprise me if they popped out a few more, so the space definitely seems to be a requirement for them. I knock on the door and wait for someone to answer.

The door swings open a minute later, and seeing no one at eye level, I shift my gaze lower to find my spunky little niece smiling up at me. "Uncle Benny!" She doesn't hesitate to run and hop up into my arms, her little hands wrapping around my neck to hug me tight.

She pulls back after a moment and scrunches her face up at me, one little finger moving to point at me in a scolding motion. "Where have you been, Uncle Benny? You haven't come to see me in over a week!"

I lean over and pretend to bite her finger, which causes her to screech and clutch onto me tighter as giggles ensue. I place a few kisses on the top of her curly blonde locks and then give her my most practiced puppy dog look. "Sorry, Gracie. I went out of town for a few days."

Her head bobs up and down knowingly. "Uh-huh. Mommy said you were getting your head screwed back on." She leans over, cupping her small hand around my ear, and whispers into it. "But I don't think I was supposed to hear that."

One side of my mouth cocks up into a half-smile as I whisper back, "That can just be our little secret then, okay?" Her head bobs up in down in silent agreement, her brown eyes wide with relief. "Where are Mommy and Daddy?"

Grace is actually Hannah's child with her first husband, my friend

106

Jackson, who I served alongside with overseas. He was killed in action shortly after I lost my leg, and unfortunately, never got to raise this beautiful baby girl. Drew married Hannah a little over a year ago and, shortly after, adopted Gracie as his own. As I look down at her adoringly, I think she may be the most beautiful creature on this planet, except for Jill of course.

I stop in my steps as I realize she's managed to creep back into my thoughts and silently curse myself. "Whattsa matter, Uncle Benny?" How are kids so damn intuitive?

I plop another kiss down on her head and smile down at her. "Not a thing, funny face. So, where's Mommy and Daddy?"

"Mommy is giving Brody a bath 'cause he pooped all over himself. It was so gross! You should have seen it, Uncle Benny. I thought Mommy was going to throw up!" She throws a hand over her mouth to try and contain her giggles.

"I think I'm glad I didn't, thank you very much!" I ruffle her hair and head toward the kitchen area. "And Daddy?"

"He's not home yet." Her mouth turns down in a little frown. She's got my brother wrapped around her little finger, and I'm sure that when he is home, she's probably got him playing dolls, or having tea parties, or whatever it is six-year-old girls do.

"Well, I guess it's a very good thing I came over then, isn't it?" I sit her down on the kitchen island and slide onto the stool next to her. I glance at my watch to check the time and then back at her. "Have you had dinner yet?"

"Nope." Her blond curls fly back and forth with each shake of her head. "Mommy said after Brody's bath."

"Well, why don't I make you something then? Grilled cheese sound okay?" I stand and wait for her response.

"Yes!" She claps her hands gleefully and bounces on the counter. "Can I help, Uncle Benny?"

I lower myself so that my face is even with hers and speak softly. "Yes, but only if you stop calling me Uncle Benny and just call me Uncle Ben."

Her brows furrow as her eyes squint in thought. Her tiny hands reach out, and she places one of each side of my stubbly cheeks, holding my face in place before speaking to me in a most serious tone. "But Daddy said you love being called Uncle Benny."

I laugh heartily, causing her to jump in surprise, a look of confusion on her face. "Your daddy is a trouble-maker, that's what he is, Gracie!"

She frowns as if this can't possibly be the case and then turns her head and smiles brightly as her mother enters the room. "Who's a troublemaker?"

"Uncle Benny said Daddy is! Does that mean he's in trouble, Mommy?" Her eyes shoot back and forth between Hannah and I, waiting for an answer.

Hannah's brow arches high as she shakes her head. "If Uncle Benny isn't careful, he's the one that's going to be in trouble."

I laugh out loud and then walk over and kiss her on the cheek in greeting. "Hey, Hannah." She gives me a quick hug and a gentle smile as she returns my greeting. "I was just going to make the doodlebug here a grilled cheese."

Her eyes open wide and turn toward her daughter. "Grace Rose Sapphire, you had a grilled cheese for lunch and for dinner last night, too. You're going to turn into a grilled cheese sandwich if you aren't careful."

"But, Mommy, I like them." She lifts her shoulders and blinks rapidly like this should be the most obvious thing ever and not a problem at all.

Hannah walks over, pecks a kiss on Grace's nose, and then lowers her to the floor. "I'll make you dinner. Go play for a little bit and I'll let you know when it's ready."

"Okay, Mommy." She smiles and waves at us both before skipping out of the room.

Hannah turns to look at me and offers me a small smile. "You doing okay?"

I nod. "Yeah, yeah, I'm good." I pace around her and move to sit back on the stool I occupied earlier. "Thank you, by the way."

She tilts her head, one brow raised in question. "For?"

"Cleaning my loft. Changing the sheets." I look down and fidget with a fork sitting on the counter. "I appreciated coming home to..." I look up at her again and shrug. "Well, you know."

Her hand falls over mine and squeezes gently. "We're family, Ben. We do what we can for each other, even if it doesn't seem like very much at all."

I look up into her soft caramel eyes and smile warmly. "My brother sure got lucky when he found you."

She shakes her head and laughs. "Well, technically, he bought me, but we won't go there tonight."

I chuckle. "Do you happen to know if there's another one like you there I could maybe look into buying?"

Her eyes darken and her smile disappears. "I think, Ben, that you may have already found what you're looking for. Maybe you just need to give it another chance?"

"Hannah, I love you, but I don't want to go there right now, okay? I came over here to try to get her off my mind. So, let's just drop it, okay?"

She sighs. "Fine, but I just want to say one thing."

I look at her, exasperation in my voice. "Do I have a choice here?"

"Not really." She shrugs like I just need to deal with it. "I just want you to know that I was at the spa the other day and saw Jill. She looked miserable, maybe even sadder than you."

"Hannah—" I try to interrupt her, but she slaps her hand over my mouth to shut me up.

"Quiet. I'm almost done." I nod and she removes her hand. "All I was going to say is that it doesn't make sense to me that two people who are so miserable apart should stay that way when they so obviously don't want to be."

I stare at her, my expression blank, and wait to see if she has anything else to add. If she slaps her hand over my mouth again, I may snap. When she remains quiet, I speak. "You done?"

She nods her head contritely.

"It's over." I move to stand in front of her and speak more quietly. "And I'm fine, okay? Or, I will be, so just drop it."

Her eyes shift to the floor, but she nods her head in acceptance. I change the subject quickly, trying to turn the mood in a better direction. "So, where's my baby brother anyway?"

"Work. Closing some deal." She looks at me and lifts her shoulders. "I didn't ask for details. But, hey, what are you doing this Friday? Want to come to dinner with us? There's a fabulous new restaurant that we got reservations for. It's called Indigenous. Have you heard of it?"

I shake my head. "Nope."

"Well, it's getting amazing reviews, and anyone who is anyone has been going, so I got Drew to snag us a table. What do you say?"

I shrug. "Sure. I'm always up for a good meal. Sounds good."

"Awesome!" She claps her hands in delight at my acceptance and I smile. Sometimes, it's the simplest things that make women happy. "Now, are you going to make those grilled cheeses? Because I'm sick of cooking them!"

I spend the next hour cooking, eating, and laughing with Hannah and Grace. She put Brody to bed after his bath, so I missed him but knew I'd see him soon. I leave around eight so Hannah can put Grace to bed, promising I'd see her again on Friday for dinner.

It has been seven excruciating days since I drove to the Hamptons to see Ben. Seven days since I left the pieces of my broken heart behind. Seven days I've been burying myself so deep into work that I have barely seen anyone.

Even at work, I stay in my office. I get there before we open, and I leave long after we close. After closing, when the cleaning crew comes in, I've been sending them home and scrubbing the place from top to bottom myself. Anything to keep myself busy and people out of my hair. I haven't even done a single treatment this week. I just can't be around anyone right now.

Aisha and Anna have been picking up the slack without a single complaint, probably because they still feel bad about what happened the last time Ben was here. I still cringe when I think about it, and when I think about the look on Ben's face when he opened the door for me in the Hamptons. How gutted he looked. I remember how badly I wanted to give everything just to take that pain away.

I shake my head. I need to stop thinking about him. I need to stop missing him. I need to accept that it is over. My phone buzzes on my desk and I glance at it. I see it's Raeva, and I know what she wants.

Mikaela and Rae have been worried about me, and they have been relentless with the well-meaning nagging. So, I let it ring. But it doesn't take long for me to realize how naïve I was for thinking that she would let that slide. Rae is tenacious when she has her mind set on something. Raeva and Mik stalk into my office, armed with boxes of Chinese food and wine. Of course, they don't even bother knocking. I look up and raise a brow.

"Come in, please. Make yourselves at home," I say sarcastically.

Neither of them seem impressed.

"I called, but you didn't bother to answer," Rae shoots back. "Now eat."

She places a couple of take-out boxes and some chop sticks in front of me. I know better than to argue with her when she uses that tone of voice. It's her stern nurse voice, and let me tell ya, she knows how to use it. I open the first box and shovel some food into my mouth. I'm sure the food is amazing, but I don't even taste it. Mikaela fishes a corkscrew out of her bag and opens a bottle of wine. My two besties sit on the chairs across from me, and for a while, we just sit and eat in silence.

"Do you remember my new friend Mackenzie?" Mikaela asks me.

I nod. "The chef?"

"That's the one," Mik says with a smile.

"Well," Rae continues. "We are planning a little dinner tomorrow night for River, to celebrate the new program he designed. And we are having it at Indigenous—Mackenzie's place."

"I really am too busy, but thanks for the invite."

Mikaela rolls her eyes. "Oh, please. Too busy doing what? Wallowing in your own sorrow?"

"I'm not wallowing. I am trying to run a business."

"A business that will run just fine without you, while you go out for dinner, particularly because you close around that time anyway."

I realize how lame my excuse is the second it rolls out of my mouth. Leave it to my friends to call me out.

"River really wants you to come. You know he adores you and hates our dinner parties. He says it'll be bearable with you there."

I groan. Of course, she is trying the guilt trip ploy. The last thing I want is to go out in public and entertain people. But, River has always been like a little brother to me; the two of us are thick as thieves. He is brilliant, dresses quirky, and makes me laugh. Maybe, hanging out with River for a night is just what the doctor ordered. Rae and Mik stare at me expectantly.

"Okay," I concede. "I'll go."

"Good," Raeva tells me smugly.

"I'm picking you up from work at five-o-clock sharp. I have dresses for us, and we need time to get ready," Mik says enthusiastically.

She gets really excited about clothing, and she should; her designs are amazing. Mikaela Kingsley is a design queen. Clothing, interior, she does it all. In fact, she did the design for her friend's restaurant. I've not seen it yet, but I am excited to see her work. I know picking me up and dressing me is a guarantee to make sure I don't cancel last minute, but I appreciate the gesture. I muster up a smile.

"Okay. I'll be ready."

"Good girl," Rae says as she refills my cup. "You've earned some more wine."

Mikaela smirks at Rae's joke, and I roll my eyes. When I look at my friends and see how much effort they are putting into making sure that I am okay, it fills me with warmth.

"Hey, guys?"

"Yes?" they say in unison.

"Thank you."

"What's family for?" Rae tells me.

"Cheers to that!" Mik chimes in.

CHAPTER ELEVEN

I take the elevator from my loft down to the lobby and walk into the brisk night air to wait for Drew and Hannah. They texted a moment ago and told me they were on their way. I glance at my reflection in the glass window from the lobby and note that what I've worn definitely reflects my mood. I'm dressed completely in black. Black Prada suit, black dress shirt, and black shiny shoes. *All the better to go with my black heart.* I shake my head in defeat over how I feel as of late.

Before I can mull over it any further, a sleek black—*how fitting*—Escalade pulls up to the curb, the window lowering to reveal Drew, a smirk on his face. "Looking for a date?"

I walk to the vehicle, open the door, and step inside to sit across from Drew. "If I was, you certainly wouldn't be my first choice."

"No, I don't suppose I would," he drawls back at me, brow raised knowingly.

I shift my gaze to Hannah, who looks radiant, dressed in a striking blue dress, her long blonde hair falling in waves around her shoulders.

"You look stunning."

"So do you!" Her eyes sweep over me quickly. "I like you in black, Ben. Very dark and sexy."

"Uh-um." Drew clears his throat and tilts his head in his wife's direction, brows creased. She turns her attention to him and smooths a hand down his chest, over his waist, and then rests it on his thigh. "Do you really need me to tell you that I think you're the most gorgeous man to walk this earth, honey?"

One side of his mouth cocks up before he leans over and presses his lips against hers for several seconds. When he pulls away, she lets out a soft breath. "Nope, but I don't want you admiring anyone else either, my love."

While I'm happy my brother is so completely in love, it's difficult not to be irritated. It feels like I came so damn close to having this same thing within reach, but instead of holding tight, I foolishly loosened my grip, any chance of love slipping through my fingers.

"I'd be happy to get another ride if you two would rather be alone." My tone is snarky, but hey, so is my mood.

"Sorry, Ben," Hannah offers, moving her hand from Drew's thigh and placing it in his hand instead. "We'll behave. I promise." She smiles and gives me a playful wink that makes it difficult for me to stay grouchy.

We chat about dinner at our parents' the following week, moving on to what the kids are dressing up as for Halloween, and then we seem to be at the restaurant. We exit the luxury vehicle and move forward to enter the restaurant. When we walk through the doors, I stop in my tracks and practically get hard. The front of the restaurant boasts a whiskey bar unlike any I've seen before, and I know instantly Indigenous may have just become my favorite restaurant.

I tap Drew on the shoulder and then point to the bar. "I'll meet you at the table. I want to see what they have to offer."

"Ten minutes, Ben." He looks in the direction our table seems to be in. "Don't make me come looking for you."

"Ten minutes." I nod my understanding. I make my way to the bar, pick up the whiskey menu sitting on its surface, and begin browsing. The choices are magnificent, making it difficult for me to decide what to choose, but it also gives me even more reason to come back again. I finally decide on a glass of Highland Park, the Ice edition, and my mouth waters to taste one of the rarer single-malts to be had.

The bartender places the glass in front of me, and I lift it to my lips, pausing when I notice some familiar faces breeze through the door. Mika and Raeva, along with Mikaela stop at the hostess station for only a moment and then carry forward into the restaurant, not noticing my presence. I make a note to stop and say hi to them when I find my table. I bring the glass to my nose, inhale deeply, and my mouth waters as I take a slow sip, drawing just a taste into my mouth. I close my eyes to savor the taste but blink my eyes open when I think I hear a familiar voice.

I turn in the direction of the doorway and freeze when I see who it is. Of course, where Raeva and Mik go, Jill is sure to follow. My heart starts to gallop in my chest as I question whether I should go over and say hello or leave her alone, which is very much what I told her I would do. I stare at her, my eyes raking down her body to admire the very short dress that displays every curve on her perfect body, down her bare thighs and to the black suede knee-high boots she's standing in, making her legs impossibly longer than the already are. *Fuck it.* There's no way I'm not saying hello.

I take my drink in hand and begin to stroll in her direction but pause again when I see the expression on her face change to relief and then joy as a strangely dressed man bursts through the door and waves her purse in the air. "Found it!"

She meets him halfway and throws her arms around him, depositing a kiss to his cheek as she does. "Oh, River, you're my hero! Thank you!"

I'm once again frozen in my tracks, my eyes glued to the scene unfolding before me. I can feel my pulse throbbing in my neck and the flow of my blood roaring in my ears. Who the fuck is this asshole? And what in the goddamn hell is he wearing? A fucking Hawaiian shirt? Under a suit that I know cost easily over a thousand dollars? This is what Jill is trying to replace me with? And what is he, twenty? He looks like a baby compared to her.

Before I have a chance to respond or move forward, he sweeps his arm around her shoulders and ushers her into the restaurant. I know my ten minutes is up, and if I don't get my ass to our table, Drew will be on the war path. Wasting what should have been a savored drink, I raise the glass of Highland Park to my mouth and down it like a shot. I walk forward, setting the glass on a table as I pass, and enter the dining room to look for Drew and Hannah.

I don't have to go far. And, *Jesus fucking Christ*, can this night get any goddamn worse? As I move closer, I see Hannah instructing a busboy to merge some tables so that we can all eat together as one large party. I scrape my hand down my face, trying to gather some sense of calm, and approach tentatively. When I'm standing beside Drew, who happens to be looking at me with a 'don't fucking ask me' expression on his face, Jill finally notices my presence, which is made obvious when her mouth falls open wide, and the grip on her date turns white.

"What the fuck, Drew?" I growl under my breath.

He shrugs. "The Kingsleys walked in, we started talking, Hannah invited them to join us, and here we are." He throws a quick glance in Jill's direction and then back at me. "This was obviously *before* Hannah realized Jill was with them."

"I thought this was just going to be a quiet dinner," I growl again.

"Then leave, Ben. No one is forcing you to stay," he snarls right back.

I turn toward him, fire blazing in my eyes. "You think I'm going to leave her here alone with that little fucking prick over there?" I cock my head in Mr. Aloha's direction. "No fucking way."

"Then sit the fuck down and shut up." He walks away to rejoin Hannah, effectively ending our conversation.

"Ben," Hannah calls to me. "Come sit here next to me." She pats the chair next to her, a look of apology in her eyes. I nod and move behind her and then slide into the seat she's offered. I lift my head, and my heart stutters when I find a pair of stormy gray eyes staring back at me, as wide with disbelief as mine.

I purse my lips but know I have to be a gentleman, even though my inner caveman is bursting to come out, and force a small smile. "Jill." I nod curtly in greeting.

She offers me a small smile in return and replies, "Ben."

My eyes shift to her right as the man-child she arrived with sits down next to her and drapes an arm across her shoulder. "This okay, Jillybean?"

She nods her head, her eyes darting from him to me, and then back to him again. He's not a complete moron because he obviously notices the tension between us and raises slightly out of his seat to extend his hand to me. "I don't think we've met. River Ray."

I stare at his hand, one I could easily crush in mine, and then raise mine off the table and grasp his. I give it a quick shake and then release it quickly so I don't unintentionally follow through with the dark thoughts running through my mind. "Benjamin Sapphire."

I think I see him falter for a moment as he glances at Jill, but can't be sure, because his movements are as smooth as glass. "I've heard a lot about you, of course. It's nice to finally meet the man in the flesh."

I quirk my eyebrow up, shifting my gaze back and forth between him and Jill and then finally respond. "Unfortunately, I can't claim the same about you. River, you said?" There is no way I'm letting this guy think he's anything but a passing fucking thought in my brain. "What do you do for a living?"

He reaches out, grabs a piece of the fresh bread that was just delivered, butters a slice, and then takes a bite. He shrugs, a smug look on his face as he responds. "A little of this and a little of that."

Without a care in the world over whoever this fucking man-child is, I turn my attention back to Jill and cock my head in a show of disbelief. "Perhaps you should teach him to not talk when his mouth his full. I mean, really, Jill, are you sure he's even old enough to drink?"

Her eyes squint dangerously, and then her red painted lips move to form a sinister smile. "Oh, don't you worry, *Benny*, he more than old enough to drink. In fact, he could probably teach an old dog like you a few new tricks."

"I highly doubt that boy could teach me anything." I snort, looking over at her date again, scanning my eyes over his lean frame, and then bring my gaze back to hers. "But if you need a reminder of what I do and don't know, Jill, I'd be more than happy to show you." I run my thumb over my lip, darting my tongue along its tip as I do, a subtle reminder of just what I can do, and chuckle when I see her cheeks flush pink.

She rises abruptly from her chair, tossing her napkin to the table, and excuses herself before stalking in the direction of the bathroom. Her man-child rises to follow, but I reach across the table and grip his arm in warning. "Stay. I'll go after her. I'm sure I owe her some kind of apology now."

He nods curtly and slides back down into his seat. "Just stop being a dick, man. She deserves better."

I meet his eyes for a moment and nod, knowing he's right, and then stride after Jill. Instead of going to the restroom, though, she walks to the entrance of the restaurant and steps outside. By the time I follow after her, she's walking in long strides back and forth in front of the building.

When I exit, she stops, spins on her heel, and marches up to me, her finger spearing me in the chest as she begins yelling. "Just who the hell do you think you are, Benjamin Sapphire? You have no right. None! How dare you insult my friend like that, and then blatantly come on to me in front of the entire table!"

I open my mouth to speak, but she stabs her finger into my chest again. I know I shouldn't feel this way, but seeing her angry like this only makes me realize how much I want her. She's so goddamn sexy when she's trying to be tough with me. "No! I don't want to hear one word you have to say! I've heard enough out of you!"

"You know what, Jill?" I pluck her tiny hand from my chest, wrap it in mine, then push my body against hers, backing her up until she's pressed up against the brick wall of the building. I take her other hand and press it above her head on the wall, stepping forward into her body so mine is completely flush with hers, making sure there's no question about how I feel. "There's not a goddamn thing I want to say to you anyway. But I sure as fuck know what I want to do to you." Before she can say another word, I slam my mouth against hers in a kiss. I kiss her until I feel her knees weaken underneath her, and her chest is rising in short pants against mine. I kiss her until I feel her hand grip onto the back of my neck and her fingernails dig into my skin. I kiss her until I finally feel her soften under me, and only then do I let her go.

We both are breathing hard and staring at each other in confusion. "Jesus Christ, Jill. What the fuck are you doing to me?" I rake my hand through my hair and then shake my head to try to clear it. I take a step closer and cup her face in my hand, a feeling of regret washing over me. "I'm sorry. So fucking sorry." And then I turn and walk away from her, fleeing the restaurant and her as quickly as I can.

Jill 3 hours ago....

As promised, Mik shows up at five sharp in one of the Kingsley vehicles to pick me up. I am under no illusion that I have any say regarding any of this, so I am ready and waiting at ten minutes to five for her to arrive. As soon as I'm home, I'm ordered to my bedroom to take a shower to get prepped. After I dry my hair, I shrug into a robe and head to Mikaela's room, where I also find Rae, both of them in Mik's dressing room.

Raeva has a ton of clothes. I mean, being married to a Kingsley has that very awful side-affect. Believe me when I tell you her closet is impressive and would earn the envy of any woman. Her closet looks like a tiny house compared to Mikaela's. I've been in here numerous times, but I still am in awe every time I step in here.

"Champagne?" Rae asks as she holds a glass out for me.

I gratefully accept. If I am going to be any fun tonight, I need a little buzz.

"Look what I got for you," Mikaela says in a sing song voice.

She holds out a beautiful leather dress that has thousands of little spots in a variety of colors painted atop of it. It almost looks like dragon skin; it's beautiful. I tell her so and she beams.

"Put it on," she says.

I eagerly accept the gorgeous garment and slip it over my head. Raeva helps me zip up while Mikaela stands in front of me, appraising her masterpiece. She claps her hands together and squeals with glee. I think she approves. Her reaction makes me giggle, and I realize that I have just laughed my first genuine laugh in a week. Maybe tonight is indeed exactly what I needed.

"Oh!" Rae exclaims. "I have the perfect boots to go with these. Be right back."

She runs off to her own penthouse to get them, leaving me with Mikaela.

"I can't tell you how happy I am to see you smile, Jill."

"It feels good to smile."

I sit at Mik's dressing table, and she positions herself behind me and starts to brush my hair.

"I know how it feels." I look up at her in the mirror. I know that she does, even though she never speaks about it. "And I understand why you walked away."

She searches for my gaze in the mirror and captures it. "I just hope that Ben doesn't turn out to be your Eric, your one and only, because I wouldn't wish this feeling on anyone. Pining for the one man you know you can never have. Knowing that no man will ever understand you the way he does, will truly see who you are. I love you, and I don't want that for you."

A tear rolls down her cheek. I rise to my feet and pull her into a hug. "Hey," I tell her. "No crying allowed, remember. This is supposed to be a fun night." I pull back enough so that I can wipe the tear from her cheek with the back of my hand and then pull her into another hug.

"Can't I leave the two of you alone for one freaking second?"

Mikaela and I share a look, and she holds her hands up. "My bad." She smiles in apology at Rae. "We're good now."

Raeva nods and then holds up her phone. "River just texted that he's headed this way, so we need to finish getting ready."

Raeva approaches me and whispers in a conspiratorial tone, "I am making him wear a suit."

I scoff. "No way."

"Yeah way."

I laugh. "Now, this, I have to see. Let's finish up, girls!"

When we get downstairs, both Mika and River are standing in the lobby, their backs facing us. The first thing I notice is, not only did River get a haircut, but he is in fact actually wearing a freaking suit. When he turns around, though, I'm pleased to see the River we all know and love is still present.

"River! You promised," Rae says with a wrinkled nose. He holds his hands up in defense. "Hey. I held up my end of the bargain. You said wear a suit. I am wearing a damn suit. I even wore the suit you sent over."

I chuckle. Typical rebellious River. He's right, of course; he is wearing a suit—a very nice one at that—only instead of a dress shirt, he has paired it with the loudest Hawaiian-print shirt known to man. He cracks me up. I walk over to him and kiss his cheek.

"I, for one, think you look fantastic," I state in support.

River beams at me. "That's because you have excellent taste, my friend."

And, with that, we walk outside and all pile into the silver Lincoln that is waiting at the curb. River blows out a long-drawn whistle. "Fancy ride, brother-in-law. New toy?"

"Are you in the market for a new toy, brother-in-law? Because I can set you up with my toy store," Mika says dryly.

"Boys and their toys," Mikaela says as she rolls her eyes.

Everyone happily chats and jokes during the short ride to Indigenous. When we pull up to the curb, I'm the last one to climb out, River waiting to assist me. We step into the restaurant, and I notice my hands are empty and slap myself on the forehead. "Crap, I left my purse in the car. I'll be right back," I say as I turn to leave.

"Don't be silly, I'll get it." Before I can even respond, he's already shot back out the door in search of my purse. I linger at the hostess' stand for only a few moments before the door opens again, and River steps in waving my purse. I do a little dance as I make my way over to him and throw my arms around him, placing a kiss on his cheek in thanks.

"Oh, River, you're my hero! Thank you!" I beam.

"You're very welcome." River slides his arm around my shoulder to lead me into the restaurant, where we spot our table mates quickly.

Only, it seems that we now have a few more guests in our party. Drew and Hannah Sapphire are also here, and the girls are working to have our tables joined for dinner. A pang of pain flinches through me, followed by relief when I realize Ben doesn't seem to be with them.

I move to greet Hannah and introduce her to River. I ask where Drew is, and she points somewhere behind me. I turn around to wave at Drew, and that's when I see him. The entire planet spins and falls off its axis, making it feel like the room is spinning out of control. I can feel the color drain from my face as my jaw goes slack. *What the fuck is he doing here?*

My first instinct is to run as my eyes dart to the exit. But, no, I can't let him see that he affects me in any way. I don't want him to think he has power over me, even though I know the truth. *Damnit, he totally does.* I'm not sure if he's noticed me, but everyone starts to take their seats, and of course, by some damn misfortune, the only two chairs available are directly across from Ben and Hannah. To make matters worse, when River pulls my chair out for me, he reaches for the one directly across from Ben.

What am I supposed to do, act like a child and tell him I don't want sit across from the mean boy that broke my heart? Ugh, that's not even accurate because he doesn't even know he broke my heart. I plaster a smile on my face, thank River, and then gracefully sink into the chair. I can't help myself, but my eyes are fixed on Ben to gauge his reaction. I can't believe my heart is betraying me like this; beating out of control, as if she is trying to escape from my chest and jump into Ben's arms. He looks up and our eyes finally connect. The look on his face speaks volumes; he doesn't want to see me at all. And fuck me if that doesn't hurt like hell, especially after the curt greeting he gives me.

River sits next to me and puts his arm around my shoulder. He knows I always get cold in restaurants. He gestures up, and my eyes follow, noticing the vent blowing cold air above our heads. I see now why he chose this seat for me. He's the one directly under the vent. "This okay, Jillybean?"

I nod my head. I seem unable to keep my eyes from wandering back to Ben. It's as if he is silently calling for me. Or am I making this shit up in my head? I'm not sure what Rae has told River about Ben, but I do know that River can scoop out a situation like no other. He introduces himself to Ben, and I get a real strange vibe from the interaction. There is definitely some kind of silent pissing match happening between them, with me being the object of their attention, which is a ridiculous thought. Ben is the one who stated he wanted to keep things professional between us. Ben looks at me and cocks his head, a look of contempt marring his chiseled features.

"Perhaps you should teach him to chew with his mouth closed and not talk when his mouth his full. I mean, really, Jill, are you sure he's even old enough to drink?"

Are you fucking kidding me?

I narrow my eyes as my temper tries to get away from me, smiling in an attempt to disguise my anger. "Oh, don't you worry, *Benny*, he's more than old enough to drink. In fact, he could probably teach an old dog like you a few new tricks."

He scoffs. "I highly doubt that boy could teach me anything." His lip rises in a sneer.

Dick.

"But," he continues, "if you need a reminder of what I do and don't know, Jill, I'd be more than happy to show you."

I can't believe he actually just said that. I'm so pissed. I sit and stew for a second, watching as he takes his thumb and traces it sexily over his lip, his eyes locked on mine. When he sees me looking, he chuckles. He's such an ass, and I've had enough. I rise to my feet, deposit my napkin on the table, and grab my purse.

"Excuse me, please."

I intend to just go to the ladies' room, but I am so angry I know I need more than just a moment. When my gaze falls on the exit door, I make a snap decision. "Fuck it," I mutter angrily under my breath.

When I get outside, I realize the car has left. Dammit. I pull out my phone and order a cab. Impatiently pacing on the sidewalk, I wait for my ride when Ben storms out of the restaurant and stands in front of me, forcing me to stop pacing. And I just snap. "Just who the hell do you think you are, Benjamin Sapphire? You have no right. None! How dare you insult my friend like that, and then blatantly come on to me in front of the entire table!"

He opens his mouth, but I don't want to hear a damn thing from him anymore. I am over it. Done. And I tell him so while poking him in the chest.

"You know what, Jill?" he says as he grabs my hand. He towers over me and closes the distance between us. I try to retreat, but not out of fear; I am not scared of Ben. No, I back up out of self-preservation. Because even though this man has just acted like a gigantic twat bucket, my body screams for him. I want him. Suddenly, there's nowhere else to go. The brick wall that is halting my escape is pressing against my back. Ben pushes against me, and I can feel how hard he is. I swallow, raising my eyes to find his blazing ones staring back at me.

"There is not a goddamn thing I want to say to you anyway. But I sure as fuck know what I want to do to you."

The next thing I know, his lips slam against mine and my world spins out of control. Just when I think my legs are going to collapse under me, he pulls away and looks at me in confusion. Before I can even gather my wits, he's apologizing and then walking away.

I watch in a daze, unable to react. *What the fuck was that?* How could he kiss me like that and then tell me he regrets it? You don't kiss someone like that and regret it. No way. Benjamin Sapphire owes me some answers, and I am going to go get them.

CHAPTER TWELVE

What the fuck did I just do? I tell her we need to keep things professional and then act like a jealous school boy the moment I see her with a man—okay, I still contend he's a child—on her arm? My strides are long and heavy as I walk away, afraid to look back, because I'm not sure I'll be able to stop myself from turning around and dragging her back home with me if I look at her one more time. Why does she have to be so goddamn beautiful, so smart, so irresistibly challenging?

I head closer to the curb so I can hail a cab and am happily surprised, and extremely relieved, when I see the Escalade pull up beside me and the passenger window sliding down. David, Drew's right hand man, is leaning toward the window. "You want me to take you somewhere, Benjamin?"

I nod and move to the back door to open it and then settle myself inside the vehicle. "Thanks, appreciate it."

"That's what I'm here for, sir." He pulls smoothly out into traffic and then meets my eyes in the rearview. "Where can I take you?"

I scrub my hand over my rough beard, wondering momentarily if it's time for me to actually shave it, and then shrug. "Home, I guess. I don't think I'm going to be good company for anyone tonight."

"Home it is." Minutes later, we arrive in front of my building, and I help myself out of the back seat and slam the door shut behind me. I give David a short wave of thanks and then turn toward the front doors. I'm about to go in when my phone starts vibrating against my chest. I reach inside my jacket and pull it out, knowing already it's either going to be Hannah or Ben. I grimace when I see Hannah's name on the screen and swipe left to read her message.

-What in the world is the matter with you? How dare you treat Jill and River the way you did! I'm so mad at you right now, Ben!

I shake my head, knowing I'm going to have to go over and see her tomorrow with my tail between my legs to apologize. Because, of course, she's right. I acted like a complete asshole. My phone buzzes again, and I read the next text, a smile small forming on my lips, thinking again how goddamn lucky my brother got.

-David said he took you home. Are you okay? Call me if you need to talk.

I slide my phone back in my jacket pocket and then enter the lobby of my building, taking the elevator up to my loft. I walk in, shrug my jacket off, and walk straight to the kitchen to pour myself a drink. I think some whiskey is in order, if I do say so myself. Lots and lots of whiskey. Whatever I have to do to get Jill out of my goddamn head.

I grab the first bottle I see out of the cupboard—I have many, mostly gifts from clients and staff—and a glass, then pour myself a good four fingers of the amber liquid. Just smelling it makes my mouth water as I take a long drink and moan in relief. I head to one of the couches, pulling my shirt from my slacks, working the buttons undone as I go, and am about to sink down when the buzzer for the elevator sounds.

Shit. Maybe Hannah decided she was going to rip me a new one tonight instead of tomorrow. I must have really pissed her off. I stride quickly over to the call button and press the intercom button. "Yep."

"Ben?" I rear back in surprise when Jill's curt voice reaches my ears. She's definitely not who I was expecting.

"Jill?" I respond. "What are you doing here?"

"Let me up, Ben. I have a few things I want to say to you."

Shit. I can hear the anger in her voice and sigh deeply as I press the button to release the elevator. *This should be fucking fun.*

I set my drink down on the table and, moving to stand in front of the elevators, shove my hands in the pockets of my slacks as I wait for her. After what feels like an eternity, the doors slide open, my breath once again catching at her beauty.

She stomps her foot on the floor of the elevator, rolls her eyes, and then storms past me. "Jesus Christ, Ben! Really? Do you have to stand there and look like... like that?" She waves her hand up and down the length of my body.

I look down to scan myself and then back up at her, my brows creased in confusion. "What the hell are you talking about, Jill?"

"Argh!" She slams her purse on the table, twirls around to face me, and places her curled up little fists on her hips. *Jesus, she's fucking adorable when she's pissed.* I can't help the smirk that dances across my lips as I watch her, fascinated.

"You really have no idea, do you?" she spits out. "And wipe that smirk off your face!"

I watch as she takes a few steps closer to me, her eyes trailing down my bare chest, and then I realize what she meant. Well, fuck, I just scored a point and wasn't even trying. I take a step closer, purposely trying to invade her space, and cheer internally when I see her falter and stand in place. "Where's your man-child? Won't he be upset that you left him and came running back to me?"

I know I'm pushing my limits here, but if I don't do something to really piss her off, really make her want to leave, I'm going to do something both of us may regret.

"You are such an asshole." She stomps her foot in place again, her hair swishing back and forth as she shakes her head in anger. "First of all, *River* is a friend. He's Rae's younger brother, whom I have known since he *was* a child, so why don't you just put that jealous shit on a shelf and move on!"

My brows raise at the fact that River wasn't her date at all, and I'm immediately torn in two by feelings of relief and then embarrassment for my assumptions and behavior. She must read the emotion on my face because she doesn't wait for me to reply before continuing.

"Yes, not feeling so high and mighty now, are you, Mr. Sapphire?"

I growl and take another step toward her. "Don't call me that. You know I hate it."

She's taunting me now, because she takes a step closer, the distance between us mere inches, and tilts her head up to mine and smiles sweetly. "And I hate that you tell me in one breath that we need to keep things professional, but then you act like a jealous husband the first time you see me on another man's arm."

Her breath is coming out in short pants, the heat of it invading my nostrils every time I inhale, reminding me exactly what she tastes like. My gaze flicks to her mouth, her eyes, and then back to her mouth again. The angle of her head changes and rears back slightly, and I know she's registered what I must be thinking. I want her. I want her so fucking badly that having her this close is making it very goddamn hard not to do what every instinct in my body is screaming at me to do.

I surprise myself, and, I think, her, when I reach forward and cup her face gently in my hands and speak softly. "And that's why I said I was sorry. You deserve better than this, Jill. I'm a fucking mess. You deserve someone whole, and good, and who isn't afraid to love you the way you should be. I'm broken, Jill. Maybe beyond repair."

Her eyes crinkle as she scrunches her forehead and looks directly at me as her voice, soothing and sweet, leaves her mouth. "We're all broken, Ben. All of us, in some way. Won't you even try and give us a chance?"

I let my head fall back as I blow out a long breath, my eyes closed as I consider what she's asking me, and then bring my gaze back to hers. "I don't want to hurt you."

Her teeth clench around her bottom lip, her cheeks flushing pink as she looks up at me from under her lashes, and then release it. Moving herself closer to me, her next words come out in a whisper. "Not being with you hurts more."

That's it. I'm done. It's all I need to hear. I slide my hands behind her head as I pull her body flush to mine and finally, finally, seal my lips against hers. Her hands snake under my shirt, against my bare skin, and wrap around my back as she holds on to me. I don't care if this ends with my heart turning to stone. There is nothing I can do to stop the floodgates she's just opened.

This isn't what I came here to do. I came here to rip him a new one. But, now, all I want is to rip every last article of clothing he's still wearing off his body. His lips are on mine, his tongue invading my mouth, our breaths becoming one. My entire body is pressed tightly up against him, but it still doesn't seem close enough.

I moan into his mouth, and he responds by grinding up against me, demonstrating just how much he wants me, too. Hands are everywhere, as if neither of us can decide where we want to touch first. Ben tears his lips away, panting, his eyes locking with mine as he rests his forehead against me. *Has he changed his mind again?*

I stare back at the hazel eyes that I always seem to find myself drowning in and am rendered speechless. The virility in his disposition is the sexiest thing I have ever seen.

"If we do this tonight, Jill, no more running. I'll be yours. Every piece of my brokenness will be yours, and you... you'll be mine." He trails his lips from my forehead, slowly moving down until he's peppering my neck with small kisses and little nips. "Every last fucking inch of you will be mine. Is that what you want?" he questions.

I can't find my voice to speak. I'm too mesmerized with him, too consumed with need. So, I just nod. I tremble as his tongue slides across my clavicle. "Say it," he growls. "I need to hear you say the words."

"I do. I want that," I manage to croak.

That seems to be all he needs. In a flash, my dress is pooled around my ankles, and I stand before him in only my black lacy panties and Rae's knee-high suede boots.

"Jesus Christ, Jill. No bra? Are you trying to kill me?"

I suck my lower lip between my teeth and swing my head back and forth. "It didn't work with the cutouts on the dress." I step demurely out of the material around my feet and push Ben's shirt off his shoulders and let it swish to the floor. A mischievous grin appears on my face, and I push against his chest, indicating that I want him against the wall. He cocks his head and raises his brows in delight and willingly obliges.

Darting my tongue out, I run it quickly over my lips and look up at Ben as I sink to my knees in front of him. I undo his belt, then his button, and grab onto the metal tab of his zipper and slowly pull it down. Using my hands, I push his slacks down, making sure to pull his boxers down as well as I go. His magnificent length springs free and stands in attention in all its glory.

I wet my lips again. I want to taste him so fucking bad. I've not taken my eyes off his once, and I feel an electric spark run through me at the desire in his eyes. I smile, wrap my hands around his cock, and then slide my mouth over its wide crown. I stroke his length with my fingers as my tongue swirls around his head.

I suck, alternating between gentle and just a little rough. His hands grab hold of my hair, and he rocks his hips against my mouth. I relax my throat and take him—all of him. I don't take my irises off his when he hits the back of my throat, moaning around him instead, thrilled when I see his head finally fall back, a long groan escaping his lips. The little sounds he makes every time he slides in serves as motivation to keep going, but Ben has different ideas.

He slides out of my mouth, pulls me to my feet, and then hoists me up in the air over his shoulder. I yelp when he smacks me gently on my lace-covered bottom and then practically purr at the warm feeling that spreads after. When he reaches the bed, he tosses me onto my back, my body bouncing slightly on its soft surface, and I break out in a fit of giggles. I like this man-cave act he's displaying.

He sits on the edge of the bed, removes his prosthetic, and then rolls over on his knees and begins prowling toward me. "My turn," he says with a wicked grin on his face. He pushes my legs apart and buries his head between them. I can feel his hot breath through my panties, and I gasp. His large hands grip either side of my lacy underwear, and in one smooth move, he pulls them off, turning them into scraps.

A surprised squeal escapes from me and he chuckles. "I'll buy you new ones," he mutters before diving back down. I forget about the damn panties the second his tongue makes contact with that little bundle of joy that he seems to have zeroed in on. He sucks and nibbles and licks long strokes up and down and up and down, driving me to the brink of insanity.

His stroking stops, and I feel the heat of his mouth cover my entire core before he sucks, hard. I come off the bed, and he pushes me down with one hand. "Uh-uh, you stay put right there, baby."

His talented tongue keeps playing with my clit as he thrusts two fingers inside of me. "Yes." I nearly come right then and scream out loud. He plunges his digits in and out of me, changing directions and applying pressure that has me writhing underneath him, all the while continuing his oral pleasure. I can feel my orgasm building in the depths of my belly, and I beg for it, for the sweet relief my body so desperately aches for. "Ben, please," I whimper.

"Ben, please what?" he teases.

"For God's sake, Ben, I need to come." I gasp.

He smirks before he takes me in his mouth once more and sucks my clit roughly, and I combust on the spot, screaming his name loudly as I fall over the edge.

I hear the ripping of foil, and before I even have time to come down from my orgasm, he positions himself over my throbbing core and plunges inside of me in one smooth stroke. All of him, every last inch, fills me completely, and I finally feel whole.

He stills for just a moment and then begins to rock against me until we are moving in tandem. It feels incredible; I don't want this pleasure to ever end. Just as I think those words, he pulls out of me, and a loud yelp of protest falls from my lips.

But before I can vocalize my discontent, he grips my waist and flips me over onto my belly. In one second flat, his hands slide to my hips, lifting them, and then he thrusts his cock back into me from behind. I rock my ass back into his hips, a moan of pure bliss rolling out of me.

One hand snakes across my belly and grasps onto my breast, while the other holds on to my hip, his grip tightening as he begins to move, and I mean really move. Long moans fall from my lips as my core starts to tremble once more. I know what's coming and I want it. I want it so, so bad.

"Oh my God," I croak over and over until I explode around him and collapse forward onto my chest, my ass still in the air. He grasps my hips tighter as he starts to chase his own release, pounding into me without mercy. Inwardly, I beg for him come, while simultaneously praying he'll never stop.

I wake up tightly nested in Ben's strong arms. When I try to move, he clutches tighter.

"Don't you even think about it," he grumbles.

I chuckle. "Geez, Sapphire, I was just turning around."

He loosens his grip, and I turn to face him, wrapping my arms around him. "Good morning," I tell him with a smile.

He kisses the top of my nose. "Good morning."

"I hate to be all cliché about this, but I have to ask; what now?"

Ben rubs his nose against mine. "I'm not sure what now. All I know is that I am miserable without you, and I don't want to be miserable. "

"I was miserable without you, too," I confess.

"Then let's not be miserable together," he says, smiling.

I giggle, then tease, "Oh, how poetic."

Ben cups my face in his hands and angles my head so that I am staring directly into his eyes. "I wasn't kidding last night, Jill. You're mine now. You chose me, broken and all, and I am not letting you go."

"I need you to hear me when I tell you this, Ben," I tell him earnestly. "I am lying here naked in your arms, not just physically naked, but emotionally stripped down. For you. Just for you. I've not shared this part of me with any man before, but I want to share it with you. You may think that you are broken, but dammit, so am I. But when I am with you... Ben, when I am with you, I feel whole."

A tear rolls down my cheek. Ben leans in and kisses it away. "Well, shit."

I frown. "What?"

"Your speech just blew mine out of the water."

I roll my eyes and playfully slap him on the chest. Ben grabs my hand and brings it to his mouth. "I'm sorry for being a complete asshole last night. Can you forgive me?"

"Can you promise me it will never happen again?"

"I solemnly swear," he says dramatically.

I grin and kiss the tip of his nose. "Then, yes, you're forgiven. But you better apologize to River."

He grumbles but concedes. "I'm glad you came over to rip me a new one," he says with a smirk.

"Stop trying to beat my speech. You won't win," I admonish jokingly.

"Fine," he tells me before flipping me onto my back. "But I bet I can show you a bunch of things I am a winner at."

"Oh? Those sound like fighting words to me, Benjamin," I tell him with a smirk.

"I think I'm up for the challenge," he counters, his eyes turning dark and sexy.

I look down where his need his pressing firmly against my belly and then back up at him. "I'd say that's more than obvious."

"You better get ready then, Angel, 'cause the games are about to start."

CHAPTER THIRTEEN

Two glorious months later...

I roll over and smile when my eyes land on the angel taking up residence across half my bed. She's managed to pull almost all of the covers off me and has them wrapped haphazardly over her body, one naked leg curled over the top, seemingly holding all of the blankets prisoner. She starts out at the beginning of the night curled up against me like a kitten, and every morning ends up like this.

I move to the side of the bed, fit my prosthetic on, and then rise silently, glancing at the clock. It's still early, just a few minutes after seven in the morning. Then I smile again because I remember what day it is. It's Christmas, and I couldn't ask for a more perfect gift to wake up to on this day. To have her here in bed every morning when I wake up is still a surprise to me.

But here she is, like she has been almost every single morning since our blow-out at Indigenous back in October. Every single fiber of my being wants to force myself back under the covers and wake her up in a way that will never have her thinking about Christmas morning

BREAKING BENJAMIN

the same way again, but I don't. We were up late last night celebrating with Mika, Raeva, and Mikeala, and I know we have another busy day ahead of us, so I tiptoe out of the enclosed space and head toward the kitchen.

When I reach the room, I press a button to open just the kitchen window shades and stare in wonder when I see the sky outside. Large, fluffy snowflakes are floating down through the air, landing on every available surface to create an enormous blanket of white. I walk closer to the window to marvel at its simple beauty, my heart filling with joy at everything I have to be thankful for today. I've always thought New York City was beautiful, but witnessing the scene before me leaves me stunned.

Warm hands wrap around my waist from behind, and I sigh as Jill presses her body up against mine, her head resting on my shoulder. "Good morning, handsome."

"Merry Christmas, my Angel." I turn in her arms and cup her face in my hands, placing a kiss on her lips. "I was trying to let you sleep. I'm sorry if I woke you."

She smiles up at me and leans forward to press her lips against mine again. "You didn't. I had to pee." She giggles and then pushes her body against mine in a hug. "And, Merry Christmas to you, too, babe."

I hold her against me, close my eyes, and savor this simple moment with her. It doesn't last long because she pushes against me and does a little hop-dance move in front of me, her hands clapping together. "Do we finally get to open presents?"

I throw my head back as I laugh out loud and then beam down at her. "How old are you, Jill Baldwin? I don't even think Gracie gets this excited."

"Ben," she drawls out in frustration, "you've been making me

142

stare at wrapped presents under that tree for two weeks. I can't take it anymore!"

I bend down, peck her on the nose, and deliver a slap to her backside that causes her to jump out of reach with a squeal. "Well, my little impatience, you're going to have to wait ten more minutes because this man needs coffee."

"Ugh." She scampers over to the coffee maker and begins preparing a pot for us, looking over at me while she does, and sticks her tongue out. "Fine, but only because I desperately need a cup, too."

I grab creamer for her out of the fridge and place it on the counter near her, dropping a kiss on her head as I pass, and then continue past to pull two mugs out of the cupboard for us. I hand them to her, and she scoops one sugar and some of the cream in a mug, leaving the other as is. We've developed an easy routine that I, for one, never in my life imagined would happen for me.

"Do you want me to open the rest of the shades, or leave it a little dark so we can enjoy the lights on the tree?"

"Open!" she exclaims with glee. "I want to watch the snow falling. It's so pretty!"

The coffee is almost done brewing, so she fills both mugs before carrying them over and handing one to me. We move in unison to the tree and, without words, both sink to the floor in front of it, looking at the lights twinkling above us, and then smile.

"Ben?" Her voice is soft and quiet as she says my name.

"Yes?"

"This is so beautiful, and it's so romantic, but if you don't let me open a present right this minute, I swear I'm going to scream."

I chuckle and set my coffee on the floor beside me. "Oh, my little Angel, always so anxious." I reach under the tree, pluck out the first gift I have for her, and place it in her eager little fingers.

Her eyes light up, just like a kid on Christmas morning, and she rips into the packaging, tearing it to shreds as she does. She's left with a flat, 8 x 10 box, which she spins around in her hands a few times, shakes, and then finally tears open. She flips the tissue paper open and pulls out the envelope laying inside, her brows creasing in curiosity as she looks up at me.

She lifts the fold and then pulls out the contents, revealing two plane tickets. I wait a minute as she reads the destination, and then grin broadly when she looks up at me, her eyes wide with wonder. "Bora-Bora?" She looks back down at the tickets again as if she can't believe they are real, and then back up at me. "You're taking me to Bora-Bora?"

I nod enthusiastically, so fucking content that she's happy with my gift. "I overheard you talking with Rae one day about your dream vacation, so..." I shrug and point to the tickets. "Because, baby, I want to make all your dreams come true."

She drops the tickets and lunges herself against me, her arms wrapping tightly around my neck as she hugs me. "Thank you, thank you, thank you, Ben." She pulls her face back enough to press her lips to mine for a few seconds, delivering enough passion to make me want to drag her back to the bedroom, and then pulls away to look at me. "You are seriously the most amazing man I could have ever hoped for."

I kiss her now and pull her back into my arms for another hug. "You deserve this and so many other things I intend to give you, my Angel."

When we release each other, I can see she's blinking rapidly, but don't worry because I know it's happiness. I've given this to her, and it fills me with a peace like none I've ever known.

She reaches under the tree to grab a present for me, but I hold up my hand. "Wait, I've got one more for you."

Her mouth falls open and then just as quickly, closes and forms a smile. "I was going to complain, but no, if you want to give me more presents today, I'll take them." She's bouncing up and down, her legs under her, and holds out her hands for another offering.

I laugh and then reach under the tree again to pull out a smaller box, wrapped in pretty gold, sparkling paper and place it in her wiggling fingers. Again, no hesitation, just ripping, the paper sitting in shreds on the floor in seconds. She holds it up to her ear, shakes it lightly, and then lowers it into her lap, lifting the cover off the small, square black box.

She gasps when the lid is off, her hand flying to cover her mouth, her wide eyes jumping up to lock onto mine. Her hand slowly lowers from her mouth, and my name rolls quietly from her lips. "Ben..." Her gaze shifts back to the box and then to me again. "This is beautiful."

I reach over, slide the box from her fingers, and run my fingers lightly over the contents. "I had this made just for you." I lift the necklace out of the box, undo the clasp, and then lean forward to secure it around her neck. It's a delicate gold chain, and on the end, her name has been spelled out in diamonds. It looks stunning on her.

"The first time I ever laid eyes on you, it was in a dazzling gold dress covered in a million diamonds." I move my gaze from the necklace to look down into her eyes, now even more moist, and offer her a warm smile. "You were the most stunning woman I had ever seen, but you wouldn't tell me your name."

She laughs and nods her head at the memory. "I remember, Ben. But, to be fair, you were insanely sexy looking and that scared the crap out of me."

I chuckle and pull her hand into mine. "This is just my way of honoring you, your name, and everything you mean to me. I'm so fucking thankful and happy you're in my life, Jill."

"Oh my God, Ben, me too." She throws herself in my arms again, this time delivering a kiss that has me dragging her onto my lap, our breathing turning heavier as it grows more heated. I'm about to lower her to the floor when she rips her lips from mine and shakes her head back and forth.

"Not yet!" She scoots herself off of me and wags her finger at me. "You are so naughty, which normally I like." She grins wickedly. "But, first, you have to open your presents!"

Today, Ben is seeing an entirely different side of me. Even though I am a respectable, well mostly, grown ass woman three-hundred and sixty-four days per year, on Christmas morning, I literally turn into a little kid. Christmas is my very favorite day of the year. I love everything about it. Spending the day with all your loved ones, eating amazing foods, hanging out in the most majestic decors... and then there are, of course, the presents. Who doesn't love presents? Not only do I love getting them; I love giving them even more. And, this morning, I'm particularly excited to give Ben his.

"Okay, are you ready?" I ask giddily.

He smirks as he kisses my forehead. "Yes, my Angel."

"It's not much," I say shyly.

"All I need is you."

After all the amazing gifts that he has just given me, I feel a little silly. I hand him a hand-carved square wooden box. It's secured shut with a tiny padlock. Ben pulls at it for a moment before looking at me with his brow raised. I chuckle and hold up the key. He reaches for it, but I pull it away. "Uh-uh, you have to listen to the story attached to this gift first," I direct with a smile.

He pulls me toward him, and I nestle up against him. "Well, let's hear it then."

"So, my grandmother and I were very close. When I was younger, she used to tell me this story about an insanely rich woman whose heart was broken and bruised by several men. The woman became jaded and scared to love. One day, she decided she'd had enough and carved a heart from the wood of a hickory tree. She cut out her own heart and replaced it with the wooden heart. She believed that, this way, nobody else would be able to hurt her heart or bruise it, because it was made of the hardest wood."

I turn my head to look at Ben and find him staring down at me with adoration. I feel my cheeks warm just from this single look and look away so I can finish the story. "One day, she meets a man, and this man didn't want her money. He didn't want her jewels. All he wanted was her love, but she was afraid she couldn't show her love because her heart was now made of wood. So, to show him that she loved him, she took her wooden heart and presented him with it, knowing he would always care for it and for her."

Now that I've shared the story with Ben, I become nervous and avoid looking him in the eye. I reach out to tentatively hand him the key and watch as he opens the box. There, on a bed of purple satin, lays a wooden heart. Ben looks at it for a second, and then his eyes flash up to mine. I bite my lip.

"Does this mean what I think it means?" he asks me.

I bob my head up and down and finally meet his gaze. "These last few months have been the best of my life, Ben. I can honestly say that I have never been this happy, ever. So, yes, it means what you think it means. I love you, Benjamin Sapphire."

Ben pulls me into his arms and peers into my eyes. "Thank you for giving me the best Christmas present I have ever had, Jillian Baldwin. No contest."

"Really?"

"Really." He places a kiss on my lips and gazes into my eyes. "I'll take your heart, Jill, and I'll keep it safe, because I love you, too. More than I ever thought possible."

After opening presents and declaring our love, we spend a good chunk of time in bed. All our activity has worked up quite an appetite, and my stomach growls loudly, making me aware that I'm starving. Ben has fallen asleep, so I slip out of bed and into his shirt before tip-toeing into the kitchen. I've decided that I am making my man a full English breakfast; eggs, bacon, sausage, fried potatoes, white beans in tomato sauce, and toast.

I am in full cooking mode when a big pair of hands pulls me backwards. "Hey there, beautiful," he mutters against my neck.

"Awe. I was going to surprise you with breakfast in bed."

"Angel, when the heavenly smells coming from this kitchen reached my nose, I had to come and investigate. You know I can't resist your cooking."

"Oh, baby, flattery will get you everywhere."

He kisses my neck. "Hmmm, everywhere?"

I turn around and point my spatula at him. "Back off, you fiend. I need to be fed before you kill me. You're insatiable."

Ben picks up a piece of bacon and pops it into his mouth. "Takes one to know one."

I smile. "Touché."

I plate our breakfast and place it on the dining table. Ben is already shoveling food in his mouth before I even have a chance to sit down. The man has a healthy appetite, and I love it. I begin eating, and we sit in comfortable silence enjoying breakfast and each other's company. When I look up, I notice him staring at me. I immediately pick up my napkin and start dabbing. "Do I have something on my face?"

He chuckles. "Your face is perfect."

I throw my napkin at him. "Then why are you staring at me?"

"Because I can't believe I got so lucky, not just to have you in my life and love you, but to have you love me back."

I smile and rise to my feet, take the few steps toward him, and lower myself onto his lap. "You say the sweetest things, Benjamin Sapphire," I tell him before kissing the tip of his nose. "But, trust me, I am the lucky one."

CHAPTER FOURTEEN

Jill steps out of the bedroom, and I can't help but admire her with pride. She always looks amazing, but today, she's dressed entirely in white, and she looks more like an angel than ever. The pants she's wearing are loose and flowy like silk, and she's topped them with a soft cashmere sweater that falls off each shoulder, her entire neck area exposed, highlighting the necklace I gave her earlier.

I'm dressed for the day as well, and have on a charcoal gray, three-piece suit, sans tie of course, with a fitted white dress shirt. I walk to her and nod in appreciation. "If I didn't know better..."

She tilts her head and scrunches up her cute little nose. "If you didn't know what any better?"

I pull her flush to me and run my hand smoothly down her back. "I would swear there are wings hidden here somewhere."

She laughs and tilts her head up to me, a smile shining on her face. "And if I didn't know any better, Benjamin Sapphire, I'd think you were trying to sweet talk your way right into the bedroom again."

I grin wickedly at her and then shake my head. "As much as I would love to do that, we've run out of time. There's some place, or I guess, some thing, that I'd like to share with you." I give her a quick squeeze before letting her go, and look down at her feet, currently clad in a pair of white heels lined with silver edging, and frown. "Do you think you could humor me and throw on a pair of boots? It will make where I want to take you much easier."

Not surprisingly, she shrugs and nods her head. "Sure. Let me go see what I might have in your closet. I can't remember."

I follow her into the room and into the closet along the back wall, and slide my feet into my black leather biker boots, but I also grab a pair of dress loafers to take with me. Jill glides up beside me, a small tote bag in hand, and takes my shoes from me and stores them in the bag with hers. She looks down at her feet and clicks the heels of her boots together, then back up at me giggling. "Yee-haw." She's wearing a pair of black cowboy boots. "It's all I could find."

I chuckle and nod approvingly. "They'll do. Much better than the heels you had on anyway."

After pulling on our jackets, hats, and gloves, we take the elevator downstairs and exit into the lobby of the building. "Give me one second, okay?"

"Of course."

I unlock the door to the gym, quickly stride across the large space into the kitchen, and grab a box I've stored in the large industrial refrigerator. Then, I make my way back to Jill.

Her brows rise as she eyes the content of the box. "Um, morbid much, Ben? Wouldn't red or white roses be more fitting on Christmas?"

I look down at the bouquets of black roses stored in the box and then back at her, my lips trying to form a small smile. "I'll explain in

BREAKING BENJAMIN

the car. Come on." I offer her my hand, and we make our way out into the snow and down the alley where my car is parked. I help her into the car, ask her to hold the box, and then climb in on the driver's side.

The alley seems to have blocked the car from much snowfall, because the wipers clear what little snow is on the windshield and the back window is barely covered as I start the car and reverse out into the street. I head in the direction of the parkway and then reach over to take one of Jill's hands. She's taken off her gloves, and her hand is warmer than usual in mine. She hasn't said a thing, intuitively seeming to understand that what I'm sharing with her isn't easy for me. When she sees the direction we're headed, she turns to me. "We're going to Brooklyn?"

I nod my head and figure there's no time like the present to start explaining. "Yes, to Cypress Hill Cemetery."

Her hand squeezes mine more tightly as she looks down at the flowers and then back over at me. "The military cemetery?"

"Yeah." I grip the steering wheel a little tighter in the one hand I'm holding it with and blow out a sigh. "I go there a lot." I shake my head. "Well, probably not as much as I used to over the last few months, but always on Christmas."

"Sorry. I'm guessing that's my fault," she lets out meekly.

I squeeze her hand. "Don't apologize. You've done absolutely nothing wrong. Believe me, Jill, none of these guys would blame me one bit for blowing them off to spend a little more time with you."

"So, tell me about your friends." She turns in her seat so she can face me. "I want to know about them."

I turn my head and give her a loving smile. "Jesus, I know I just said this an hour ago, but damn if I'm not the luckiest bastard in the whole world."

152

"I'd say we both got pretty lucky." She lifts my hand to her mouth and places a soft kiss on the back of it before lowering it back to her lap.

"Well, you know, of course, about the gym, and that it's dedicated to the guys I served with. Baker and Landon were in the truck with me when we hit the explosive that took my leg. Baker was one of my closest friends, and when I woke and saw him dead next to me, it was like someone had stuck a goddamn stake into my heart. I didn't find out until after I woke up in the hospital that Landon had died as well."

I close my eyes for just a second, the pain from the memory causing my heart to contract tightly, but breathe out, trying to push it away. "I was sent home, of course. And pissed as hell, of course. Pissed my friends had died and I couldn't even go to their funerals or help their families. Pissed I lost my leg and couldn't go back and blow those mother fuckers up. And pissed that our country didn't seem to give a flying fuck about what was happening to those still over there serving."

"So, basically, you were pissed." She chuckles lightly, and I can't help but let out a laugh in return.

"Yeah, I guess that about sums it up," I state jokingly. "I think the worst of it for me, though, was Rose, er, Jackson; Hannah's husband. He was actually a Marine, not Army like me, but we were all stationed in the same area, and somehow, this squirrely little fucker got under my skin and seemed to be everywhere I was. We became friends... good friends."

"I've seen pictures of him in Grace's room. Did you know that there's one of you and him together on her dresser? You look so young in it!"

"Yeah, I actually gave that to Hannah a while back. It used to be in my office, but I don't know, it just seemed like something I wanted her to have. Hannah said she wanted Gracie to know that her daddy and her uncle were friends, so she thought her room was the best place for it." I can feel I'm starting to get a little more than nostalgic, so I shake my head to try to clear away some of its weight.

"You okay?"

Jill reaches out a hand and places it softly on my cheek. I turn my head and place a kiss on her palm and then nod. "I'm good. Just a lot of memories."

Her hand moves back to her lap, covering the one that's holding her other hand, and rests there, her fingers grazing back in forth in comfort over my skin.

"Yeah, so Jackson came back to the States on leave when Grace was born, and he came to see me. I was still in the hospital healing, still angry as fuck. He was even madder than me, and was so eager to get back and, as he put it, 'get even'. I begged him to reconsider. He just had a baby, for Christ's sake. He had a beautiful wife. He had both goddamn legs. But he wouldn't listen to reason. He died a few weeks later, killed in action."

I look over at Jill and am surprised when I see tears streaming down her face. "I'm so sorry, Ben. I wish there was some way I could take all this pain from you and carry it instead. You've lost too much already."

We're in the cemetery now, so I pull the car over and put it in park, but leave it running so the car will stay warm, and then pull her into my arms. This is why I love this woman so much. To want to take my pain and have it be her own. Who says things like that? Who wants to do things like that? She lives up to my nickname of Angel more every day. I kiss her head and whisper, "I love you so much, Jill."

"I love you right back." She hugs me hard and holds on until I slowly pull us apart.

"This helps me." I lift my hand and point a finger out my windshield toward the gravestones in front of us. "Coming here. Honoring them. Making sure they know I'll never forget them or what they meant to me, to this country."

"And the black roses?" She looks down at the box she placed on the floor between her legs some time ago.

I point to the tattoo on my arm. A few of us got these to honor Baker, Landon, and Jackson. The rose specifically for Jackson, and well, you know all about my black heart." I shrug.

"I know all about your heart, Ben, and it's nowhere near black."

I look at her and smile. "Not anymore."

She goes with me then, and we walk through the cemetery, stopping at the grave of each of my friends, my brothers, and we place a bouquet of the roses on their stones. I tell her a little more about each of them. Hannah is the only other person I've brought with me here, but Jill is the only one who has ever made my heart feel lighter while doing so.

———————

An hour later, we pull back into the alley and park the car. We run up to the loft and grab three big bags of presents and a couple bottles of wine, and then head back outside. The snow is still falling gently, so we decide to leave our boots on and just walk the block over to Drew and Hannah's place. Jill tries to catch snowflakes on her tongue as we walk, and I think my cheeks might actually crack if my smile grows any wider as I watch.

We reach the building in minutes and stomp the snow off our feet as we enter the lobby and share Christmas greetings with the doorman. He knows us by name, our familiarity a product of the frequent visits we both make here. When we step off the elevator, Gracie is already standing in the hallway waiting for us, arms thrown wide as she runs over and hugs us both.

"Merry Christmas, Uncle Benny and Jill!" I drop the bags and scoop her up in my arms, swinging her around before giving her a large hug. When I look up, I see my mom standing in the doorway to the apartment, a very content looking Brody on her hip, sucking on a green candy cane.

"Merry Christmas, Mom." I smile and set Grace on the ground so I can retrieve the bags and enter the house. I give my mom a one-armed hug and watch with warmth as Jill hugs her with both.

"You two are all covered in snow." My mom is already beginning her fussing. "Put those bags right there and take off those wet shoes and coats before you come in any further. Hannah will have a fit if you dirty up her floors."

"What will I have a fit about?" Hannah strolls in carrying a large tray of cut of vegetables, and places them down on a table before moving over to give Jill and I a hug. "Merry Christmas, you two."

She takes a step back, places a hand on her hip, and cocks her head at us. "You two are practically glowing. Any news you want to share?" She glances toward Jill's left hand and lifts her brows in hope.

Jill's eyes pop wide, and her head begins shaking back and forth. "Oh God, no! Hannah!" She slaps at her playfully and then lays her hand flat against her breast bone under the necklace I gave her. "I mean, wouldn't you be glowing if Drew had your name put in diamonds?"

That's all it takes for all three women to gather round and start chatting about presents and shoes, and whatever it is women go off and talk in circles about. I chuckle as they all head off in the direction of the kitchen, and then look down when I hear crinkling behind me.

"Gracie, what are you doing?" Her little blonde head pops out of the bag, her wide eyes meeting mine.

"Nothing, Uncle Benny. Just looking to see which presents are mine." She starts bouncing up and down in place, and I can't help but laugh out loud when I realize she's the spitting image of Jill a few hours ago.

"Well, let's go find Dad and Grandpa and see if we can't gather the troops so we can open these puppies up. Sound good?"

"You got me a puppy?" Her eyes light up as her face widens in delight, and I freeze in place.

I let out a long sigh and realize it's going to be a very long day as I try to explain my choice of words. I wonder where the hell my brother is hiding because I need to join him pronto. And, Jesus, I was ready for a damn Christmas drink, too.

We spend the next few hours opening presents, well, Gracie doing most of the present opening, and then have a wonderful dinner together. I realize as I look around the table, surrounded by the people who mean the most to me, who I love the most, that I may just be the luckiest man alive. And for the first time in a really long time, I don't feel guilty anymore for being the one that survived.

I smile over at Jill and take her hand into mine and squeeze it softly. "Thank you for the most amazing Christmas I've had in a long time."

"You're so welcome." She raises her eyebrows and smiles wide. "But the day's not over yet. You haven't seen Christmas until you've experienced it with Raeva..."

Jill, later that evening...

If there is one person who loves Christmas more than I do, it is Raeva Kingsley. Even before she had access to the best of the best, Christmas at our house was out of control. Luckily for Rae, her husband adores her and is indulgent. In fact, we all love her for her holiday spirit. Poor Ben, however, has no idea what he's about to walk into, and I barely contain my laughter when we enter the penthouse and I watch Ben's jaw almost falls to the floor.

The second we step foot over the threshold, it's as if we have stepped into a winter wonderland. There are thousands upon thousands of little white lights strewn throughout the penthouse, and everywhere you look, there are little elves. Some of them in plain sight, some of them peeking from a corner. Then, there are the countless crystal snowflakes that are suspended from the ceiling, reflecting against the white twinkly lights, and the effect is mesmerizing.

No, Rae doesn't believe in doing Christmas halfway, and even has seven, yes seven, Christmas trees, each in a different color scheme, throughout the penthouse. But the best surprise is when Rae comes running around the corner dressed in an atrocious sweater, squealing like a little school girl.

"Jillybean!" She throws her arms around me in an exaggerated hug and then remembers to address my date as well. "Oh, hi Ben!

Merry Christmas, you guys!"

I look over at Ben, whose eyes have widened, and I lose it. Raeva releases me, and after scanning us from head to toe, wrinkles her nose. "Nope," she says sternly. "This just won't do."

Ben turns to look at me, not understanding what is going on.

"Luckily for you, I'm prepared. There is a rack in my dressing room. Pick out something appropriate."

I chuckle and kiss my person on the cheek. "Yes, ma'am."

I probably should have warned Ben that this party is also Rae's annual ugly sweater shindig. But, then again, where would be the fun in that? I take his hand and lead him to her dressing room. "Come on, handsome, you heard the lady. We are not dressed for the occasion."

Ben has yet to say a word, which is so unlike him. He's clearly not in his element, and I can't deny that I draw some entertainment value from that fact. We reach Rae's dressing room, and I peruse through the rack. I find the ugliest sweater known to man and triumphantly hold it out to Ben.

"You want me to wear *that*?"

"Sure do."

Those dimples that I adore make an appearance. "As you wish." He shrugs his jacket down off his shoulders and moves to hang it on one of the available hangers on the rack. Next, he takes the sweater from me, pulls it over his head, swipes his unruly locks back from his face, and then rewards me with a cocky grin. It looks like Christmas has thrown up on his torso, but damn him, even in this ridiculous sweater, he is still the most gorgeous man I have ever laid eyes on.

"Wait," he tells me as he pulls me away from the rack. "All's fair in love and war, right? Now, it's my turn to pick yours."

I step aside and motion for him to go ahead. Ben inspects each sweater on the rack carefully before making his choice. When I see what he's chosen for me, I can't help but chuckle. "Really?"

He nods with a smirk. "Really."

I'm happy he's getting into the spirit, so I take the sweater and pull it over my head. The second I do, his lips are on mine. "You look beautiful, Angel," he tells me.

I look down at my ugly reindeer sweater with glitter and tassels decorating my chest, and shrug in defeat. "Benjamin Sapphire, I dare say that you have it bad."

"Damn right, I do."

"Good, 'cause so do I."

We kiss once more but pull apart moments later when someone clears their throat. "You two better head down before Rae calls for your heads on a platter," Mika jokes.

"Hey there, Captain."

"Captain?" Ben asks curiously.

"Don't listen to her. It a ridiculous nickname my wife and Jillybean over here came up with," Mika grumbles.

"I'll tell you later," I mouth at Ben.

"And, Ben, let me start by saying, I apologize for my wife's... um, enthusiasm. She means well, but holidays make her a little crazy."

"A little?" I scoff.

Mika and I both laugh, but Ben looks a little worried. We all head downstairs, where the moment my feet are off the last step, I get pulled aside by the girls and away from Ben. He continues on behind Mika and toward the bar.

"So, show us the necklace!" Mikaela says excitedly. Of course, I told the girls about it earlier in a group text. I reach beneath my ugly sweater and pull it out.

"Oh my God, that is stunning," Rae exclaims. Her fingers reach out and trail over the sparkling jewels sitting around my neck.

It is hard not to swoon.

"Look at that smile on your face. I don't think I have ever seen you happier than you have been over the last few months. Ben has been good for you," Rae says with tears in her eyes.

"He has," I tell my girls. "I love him, you guys."

"And he loves you, it is easy to see. The way he looks at you, like he thinks you hung the moon..." Mik tells me.

"We are so happy for you two," Rae chimes in.

The three of us hug. Both of my besties are beaming. I tell them about the Bora Bora tickets, and about the heart and the story behind it, and by the time I am done, they both are dabbing their eyes.

"Who knew that our Jillybean was such a romantic?" Mikaela jokes.

"That Sapphire guy is a lucky man. I hope he knows that."

"Now, girls, I am going to need you to take it easy on him tonight, okay? I'd like him to stick around."

Raeva gasps. "Why, Jillian Baldwin, are you saying that I am not always on my very best behavior?"

"How did you even say that with a straight face?" I say, laughing.

I look over at Ben who is on the other side of the room. He's standing in front of the fireplace, ugly sweater worn with pride, glass filled with amber liquid in hand, and smiling. After everything we shared today, that smile means even more to me. I'm grateful for his survival, because I know there isn't anyone else on the planet for me. He thinks he's broken because he's missing a leg. But what he doesn't realize that I was broken, too, because I was missing him. Finding him, loving him, and him loving me back, has made me whole.

He looks up and catches me staring. He raises his glass and winks at me. I know this ugly sweater party isn't his thing, but he is trying for me, and it makes me love him even more. He's trying to have fun and to get to know my friends, because I doubt there is anything that man wouldn't do just to put a smile on my face. So, right here, right now in this moment, I vow to myself to do the same for him...

CHAPTER FIFTEEN

One Week Later...

My eyes flutter open, and I lift my head off the pillow to look down to try to figure out what's woken me up. One side of my mouth cocks up when I see the top of Jill's head hovering over my stomach, her finger tracing over the lines of one of my tattoos. "Morning, beautiful."

She hums as she places a soft kiss against my chest. "Morning."

"Whatcha doing down there? Come give me a proper kiss," I growl, reaching down to pull her up.

"I don't think I've gotten to know this one yet." She pushes my hand away and continues moving her finger lazily over my lower abdomen.

I chuckle softly and move my hand to rest it in her hair instead. I know where this is headed, and I have absolutely no intention of interrupting her. "Angel, I think you know all my tattoos pretty well by now, but by all means, investigate further if you must."

She raises her head just enough so she can peek up at me under her lashes, licks her lips as she flashes me a very sexy smile, and then leans back over me, replacing her finger with her tongue. My head falls back against the pillow, and I close my eyes, letting myself bask in the attention she's giving me right now.

I feel her tongue lift off my skin and then the vibration of her voice as she speaks. "I don't think I ever noticed the way these feathers curve up here around this muscle." And then her tongue is back against my skin, the tip dragging along the edge of one of my lower muscles, and then lower still, my skin breaking out in goosebumps as she goes.

"Last time I checked, there wasn't any ink below my waist, love," I murmur, but don't hesitate to lift my hips when her hands make quick work of removing my boxers.

"Shhh, I'm just looking to make sure." Her fingers trail up my stomach and then rake back down slowly, stopping when they circle around the base of my cock and tighten, her tongue dragging up its hard length, and then her hot, wet mouth sliding down to cover me.

My hips thrust up involuntarily, and a loud moan rolls up from my chest. *Now, this is a great fucking way to wake up.* My hands find her head, and I tangle my fingers in her downy locks, helping to guide her up and down as she sucks me in and swirls her tongue around me, my cock growing even harder. She moans and the vibration against my cock almost causes me to explode right then and there.

I tighten my grip in her hair and pull her off me with a soft pop, guiding her back up my body. When she's close enough, I slam my lips against hers and yank her body flush to mine. She's naked, and her hard nipples brush against mine as she adjusts herself over me. She thinks she's in control, and for a moment, I let her believe it as she slides her wet center up and down my throbbing length.

When she shifts to move higher so she can impale herself with my cock, I grab her arms and roll over, trapping her beneath me, a small gasp falling from her parted mouth as her wide eyes look up at me. "You don't think I'm going to let you do that yet, do you?"

Her teeth find her lower lip and she bites it, as if trying to quench the obvious hunger stirring within, shaking her head softly. I don't give her a chance to reply verbally, because I crush my mouth to hers, my tongue twisting with hers, her body pushing back against mine in desperation. She wraps a leg around me and tries to rock her center against my cock, but I release her lips and slide down her body, effectively breaking the hold she has, and suck one taut peak into my mouth.

I smile around the nipple when I feel her hands clutch the sheets next to me and hear a moan from above. My minx is on fire, and my lips on her only seem to fan the flames higher. I release her hard bud, run my tongue over it with one hard swipe, and then rake a wet trail down her stomach until I reach the apex of her legs. Without hesitation, her legs fall open wide in invitation and I enter greedily, plunging my tongue into her sweet core. I stroke softly against her until I land against her hard nub and then wrap my lips around her and suck.

Her hands are instantly in my hair, clutching wildly, her knees rising to push her feet into the bed as I grasp her hips tightly and suck even harder. "Oh my God, Ben. I'm going to come if you don't stop."

I want her to come, I do, all over my goddamn face, but I want her pulsing around my cock even more, so I release her and move like lightening up her body and between her legs. Her hands move to my arms, her nails digging into me as she clings to me, and I lean over and slowly ease myself into her. Her hot walls clench and then pulse, pulling me in deeper, holding tightly as I arch my back and plunge all the way in.

We both groan when my center slams against her, and I still, but only for a moment before I slide back out and then drive back into her again.

"Oh my God, yes. Fuck me, Ben!" I need no further encouragement and surge back and forth against her body, thrusting my cock as deep as it will go, my arms flexed tightly as I hold myself over her. After only a few moments, I feel her tighten around my cock like a blood pressure cuff, her head thrashing back and forth on the pillow, her hands reaching out to grasp me around the neck. She lets out a long, guttural moan, followed by my name in a whisper.

As if it was even possible, hearing my name from her pink lips causes my blood to surge straight to my cock, making it even harder. I move faster now, my hips pummeling against hers as I feel my balls tighten and then finally explode, my release coating her insides. I clutch onto her, pulling her flat against me, my hot breaths against her ear as I moan out her name again and again.

When my pulse finally slows down enough for me to think reasonably, I roll off her and lay flat on my back, my breaths still coming out in pants. *Holy fuck. How in the world does this just keep getting better and better?*

She lifts herself and lays the top half of her body across my chest, her hand under her chin as she looks up at me. "Did I say good morning yet?" And then she breaks into a fit of giggles as her face flushes a beautiful shade of pink.

An hour later, we're both showered and in the kitchen. I'm drinking a cup of coffee as I watch her move around, cooking for us. She's humming and moving her hips softly to the rhythm, and I realize I could never feel more content. "Move in with me."

166

She freezes, spatula suspended in mid-air, and turns to me, eyes wide, her mouth forming a small 'O' shape. "What?"

"Move in with me." I set my mug on the counter and move closer to her. I slide the spatula from her fingers and then wrap my arms around her. "You're here all the time anyway now."

"Ben..." Her face scrunches up in thought for a second. "I mean, I don't know. What about Mik?"

"What about Mik?" I counter. "She's a big girl. And Rae is right across the hall from her. I'm quite sure she'll be just fine."

She chews on her lip in contemplation, and I can tell there are a hundred thoughts swirling around in her head. "Listen, just think about it, okay?" Her head nods up and down, her expression dazed. I pull her in closer to me. "Jill, I love you. I love having you here. I love waking up with you every day. I didn't mean to freak you out or scare you."

"I'm not scared." She peeks up at me. "Nothing has ever felt more right to me."

"Really?" I can't help the smile that spreads across my face.

"Really." She nods again, almost like she can't believe what she's saying. "I just have to figure out how I'm going to tell the girls."

"So, you're moving in? That's a yes?" I have a hard time containing the joy in my voice, but I don't give a shit. It gives me a sense of relief and anticipation knowing what else I have planned for her tonight.

Her face breaks into a huge smile. "It's a yes."

"Woohoo!" I tighten my arms around her and swing her around in a large circle, crushing my lips against hers in delight. She squeals out in laughter and then slaps at my arms to put her down.

"Ben, put me down! I have to finish breakfast." Her cheeks are flushed and I know, even though she's trying to play it cool, she's just as excited as me for this next step. "If I'm not at Rae and Mik's by eleven, they will kill me. You know how they feel about preparations."

"Well, if this is the start to our New Year, I think it's going to be fucking amazing." I plant one more kiss on her cheek and let her go so she can finish cooking. "So, what does that crazy duo have in store for you this time?"

"Oh, you know them... Of course, the entire afternoon will be spent at the spa. My rules, not theirs. There's no way I'm showing up to your charity event tonight looking anything less than fabulous."

"Angel, you could show up in a plastic bag and I'd still think you were the most gorgeous woman in the world." I slap her ass playfully and wink.

"You, Benjamin Sapphire, are biased." She turns and smiles sweetly at me. "But thank you. After the spa, we're going to go to my place for dressing. Mik has designed some stunning new creations for us to wear. I can't wait to see them!"

"And I can't wait to see you in it." I raise my brows suggestively.

"You're insatiable!" She grins back. "Are you sure you don't mind me meeting you at the event? It's just going to be so much easier riding over with Mik and the gang instead of coming all the way back over here."

I move up behind her, wrapping her in my arms, and lean my head down on hers. "I told you already, it's fine. It's good, actually, because I have a ton of stuff I need to do before the event. Need to make sure all ducks are in a row and what not."

She spins in my arms, throwing hers around my neck, and smiles up at me. "I love you, Benjamin. I know I tell you all the time, but I do. I just want you to know that. And I'm still so glad every day that you chased after my stubborn ass."

I soften at her words, knowing without a doubt that everything I have planned for this evening is happening at the perfect time. "I love you, too, Jill." And I kiss her, hoping to show her just how much.

CHAPTER SIXTEEN

After we have spent the entire day at the spa getting pampered, we arrive at the penthouse with the girls in full-blown party mode. I go to my room, take a quick shower, and then head to Mik's dressing room to see what kind of magic she's created for me. I walk in just in time to hear the cork pop.

"Jillybean!" They greet me in unison.

"Hey, guys." I stroll in wearing my robe, a smile on my face.

Raeva hands me a glass of champagne, smiling like the Cheshire cat.

"What's with the face breaking smile?" I ask with a chuckle.

"I'm just excited about tonight. Whoever came up with the idea for this party is brilliant. Oh, and wait until you see what Mikaela has got for us to wear tonight."

I don't even have to see the outfits to know that they will be spectacular. Everything Mik designs is fabulous. It's New Year's Eve, and we're going to a party being held at the new Sapphire Resort; the very one I met Ben in, which seems like such a good omen to the start of our night and the year ahead.

Someone came up with the amazing concept of working the party into a charity. Every guest must donate money into a pot in order to attend. The guests then divide into teams for a scavenger hunt, with the winning team getting to choose the charity they want the total funds donated to. Not only does it sound like fun, but we get to help a good cause.

"Is Ben meeting us here?" Mik asks.

I shake my head and take a sip of the champagne. "No, he said he had tons to take care of for the event and that it would be easier for him to just meet us there."

"Ah. Okay, well, when he sees you, he might not get up."

I frown. "I'm sorry... what?"

Mikaela rolls her eyes. "Because you'll look so amazing; you'll knock him out. Duh."

Raeva and I burst out laughing. "You're a nut, Mik."

She smirks and holds out a hanger with a gorgeous black sequin dress. The dress has a rounded neckline, with a scooping back and three-quarter sleeves. And, it's short, falling a good five inches above my knee making it incredibly sexy. Ben loves when I show some leg. Of course, it fits like a glove. Mikaela is a magician when it comes to things like this. She knows exactly what looks good on anyone or anything.

"You will need a pair of amazing shoes to go with that, of course," Rae chimes in. "Luckily for you, your person has just acquired these." She passes me a shoebox, and my brows rise in delight when I read Jimmy Choo on the box and know they are going to be fancy. I lift the lid and gasp. Inside, I find a pair of black and silver, coarse-glitter-covered, pointy toe pumps. They are perfect. I hug my friends and thank them.

I start to work on my make-up, and watch in the mirror as Rae and Mik begin dressing, all of us continuing to chat about this and that. Mikaela is wearing her signature gold. The color matches her eyes, and she looks stunning. The loose silk of the dress falls around her making her look like a goddess. The matching gold gladiator heels finish the ensemble.

Raeva is dressed in a gorgeous silk top and pant set. The print on the fabric is made up of pink and orange blossoms, and the contrast of color against the black is magical. The top ties around her back and exposes her shoulders and just the tiniest bit of her belly. The matching pants also have a tie belt, and are wide-legged and flow when she walks, making it appear that she is gliding through the air.

Yes, we look amazing, and we beam in pride at each other. I do make-up and hair for each of us. Mika must be getting impatient for our company, because he's already sent three texts in the last twenty minutes. We take the final one as our queue to leave and all rise and take one last look in the mirror.

We squeeze each other's hands and look expectantly at each other before I finally speak. "I think we're ready, girls." We all nod in agreement and leave the dressing room to head to the party.

Once downstairs, we climb into a gorgeous white limo and head to the financial district. I pull my phone out of my purse, check the screen, and frown. Still nothing from Ben. It's a bit strange, as he usually checks in, but I try not to think too much about it, knowing he had so much to do to prepare for the event. I'll see him very soon and can't wait for him to see me in Mik's latest creation.

I've been wondering all day how I am going to tell Mik that I am moving in with Ben. I know she will be happy for me, but I hate the thought of her being alone in that big place. I know I've spent almost every night since meeting Ben at his place anyway, but I still can't help but feel bad. I know she's lonely, especially in the evenings, when she's wishing she could be with Eric.

When we pull up in front of the building, a large smile breaks across my face as my mind drifts back to all those months ago—the night Ben picked me out of the crowd, my knight in shining armor, even if I didn't know it then, at the opening gala for the hotel. I shake my head when I recall my unwillingness to even have a drink with the man, and whom I now can't imagine being without.

We head into the lobby where we are all greeted and directed to the coat check. I scan the room for Ben, but still see no sign of him. We make our way to the large ballroom on the second floor as a group and all marvel at the opulence before us. The room is gorgeously decorated for the occasion with flowers dipped in glitter scattered throughout and candles burning on every surface. After securing drinks at the bar, we find our table and take our seats.

A staff member gets on the small stage in the center of the room and begins the evening by requesting our donations and then directing us to a list containing the name of our assigned team mates. Of course, because I know some strings must have been pulled, my team consists of Hannah, Mikaela, Raeva, and of course, myself.

The rules are explained again, and we each listen intently. Each team has until midnight to try to solve the clues provided to them. Each clue will lead to the next and so on until we get to the last one. The first team to get to the last clue will get to pick the charity of their choice to donate the combined money to. We are instructed to assign a team captain, and without hesitation, Raeva gets the job with a unanimous vote.

"Okay, first things first," Rae says, holding a little card. "According to this, we have to declare our charity before we start. Any suggestions?"

"Get Vets Set!" Hannah and I say in unison.

We look at each other in surprise and then giggle.

"It's Ben's charity." I explain. "He offers free gym memberships and physical therapy for vets. It is such a great initiative, and I would love it if we would support him."

"I second that," Hannah chimes in.

"I'm three for three," Mik says with a grin.

"Get Vets Set, it is!"

Raeva fills out the card and hands it in, and we receive our very first clue. It's a balloon. There are some numbers and letters written on the face of it, but they don't make sense; *P4P M2 T4 S22 WH1T C4M2S N2XT*. Attached to the balloon is a little card that says:

A = 1

E = 2

I = 3

O = 4

U = 5

We stare at the balloon and the card for a moment.

"Ohhh," Rae exclaims as she pulls a pin from her hair. "Pop me to see what comes next!" She stabs the pin into the balloon.

A little note falls out, and I pick it up, unfold it, and read it out loud. *"In order to find the next clue, you will have to go to the front desk and ask for something. To find out what to ask for, solve this riddle: I have cities, but no houses. I have mountains, but no trees. I*

HAYLEE THORNE & MICHELLE WINDSOR

have water, but no fish. What am I?"

I'm glad I've only had one glass of champagne, because apparently, we are going to need our thinking caps on tonight. I repeat the words and mull them over in my head. Then, I remember a few weeks ago, while Ben and I were visiting Drew, Hannah, and the kids, Gracie made Ben and me watch this cartoon with her. What were the odds?

"I know what it is!" I exclaim, and motion for them to follow me as I make a beeline for the front desk. The others don't hesitate and follow. When we make it to the front desk, I approach the young lady behind the counter and give her one of my brightest smiles. "Excuse me, um," I look at her name tag, "Gloria, would you by any chance have a map?"

Gloria beams and nods her head in delight. "Certainly, ma'am. Just a moment."

She bends behind the counter for just a second, and then pops up, holding a map of the hotel in her hands. She passes it over to us, and we open it, noting there is a route highlighted. We thank Gloria and start to figure out where we are on the map. We follow the highlighted path and end up in a small room with a table set up in the middle of it. The table has a beautiful hand-painted silk table cloth, and on top of the table are twelve different desserts, a pitcher of water, and a dozen water glasses. Next to the pitcher sits a little locked black box, and next to that, tied to a little holder on the table, is another balloon.

Raeva pulls the pin back out of her hair and pops the balloon. Another note drops, and Mikaela picks it up and unfolds it. *"One of these yummy desserts holds the key."*

The key? To the box?

"Well, ladies, let's dig in," Hannah says as she grabs a fork.

"I call dibs on the crème brulee!" Rae says as she lunges toward her favorite dessert with gusto.

"I'll guess I'll go for this lava cake," Mik announces.

I myself am about to dig into a huge piece of triple chocolate cake when Hannah announces that she has the key. It's covered in frosting, though, so Mikaela pours some water in a glass and drops the key in it. We fish it back out, clean it off, and then open the box. Inside the box is yet another clue.

"A woman shoots her husband, then holds him underwater for five minutes. Next, she hangs him. Right after, they enjoy a lovely dinner. Explain."

The four of us look at each other before a giggling fit ensues.

"Nice lady," Hannah chuckles.

"Oh my God, I know what this means!"

We all look expectantly at Mikaela.

"Listen, when I was in school and had time for hobbies, I used to love to take pictures. Never digital, though. I was an old-fashioned girl—except when it came to clothes, of course," she says with a wink. "Anyway," she continues, "all of it can be explained. We need to find a picture or a darkroom or both. Hannah, does this resort have one?"

"Honestly? I am not sure. The resorts are Drew's territory."

"Wait," Rae says. "The map!"

Sure enough, when we unfold the map, we find that the resort does indeed have a darkroom. We head there immediately. The darkroom is located below ground level, so we take the elevator down and are relieved to find the room unlocked. But the red light outside is on, which means we can't go in. Fortunately, there is a balloon tied to the doorknob. We pop it, and once more, a note falls to the floor, but also four keys.

"A picture speaks a thousand words. But only one key works."

Each key has a keychain on it that reads a different direction. North, East, South, and West. Hmmm. Cryptic. We knock but get no response.

"Oh, screw it," I tell my friends. "I'm going in."

My friends reluctantly follow me into the darkroom, which is just that, dark. Besides the red glow that illuminates the room, it is devoid of brightness, but we notice there are several pictures hanging from a line. I step forward and inspect the images. On every picture, there is a terrace, and it looks to be the same terrace. In the middle of the terrace, tied to something is a balloon.

"I know where this is!" Hannah says excitedly. "It's the roof top terrace. There are four entrances, and I think one of these keys will open a door. Only thing is, I have no idea which. I say, if we want to win this thing, we need to split up."

"Yes, great idea," Mikaela chimes in. "There are four keys and four of us. We will split up, and whoever opens the door first and finds the balloon will call the others. Sound good?"

I am totally good with that. I really want to win the donation money for Ben's charity. Raeva divides the keys. She gives Hannah South, Mik West, me North, and she heads to the East. We all take the elevator to the top floor before splitting up.

On the top floor, there is a small stairwell that leads to the roof terrace. I head to my particular stairwell and climb up until I reach the door. I insert the key and squeal with glee when I attempt to turn the knob and it actually works.

I push the door open and step onto the terrace. When I do, I am mesmerized, my mouth falling open at the beauty before me. There are literally an ocean's worth of white lilies and candles spread on every surface. It is absolutely breathtaking, and I marvel at it a moment in silence.

Even the chilly December wind that brushes across my skin with its icy touch isn't a deterrent, and I move forward to investigate. I walk further onto the terrace and spot the balloon. I stride toward it with tunnel vision. I stop, because I realize that I have no pin. I look at the balloon and frown for a moment. A smile tugs at my lips when I realize I have something else I can use; a pen that I stuck in my purse after I wrote the donation check downstairs. I fish it out and pop the balloon, my face lighting up in victory.

Unlike with the other balloons, this time, there is a loud thud as something drops to the floor. I look down, pick it up, and stare at it. It is a small black heart, made from some type of stone. I'm turning it in my hand when I'm startled by a familiar voice behind me.

"My Angel, so resourceful."

I turn and see my gorgeous man sauntering toward me. He is wearing a three-piece black suit that is so perfect on him that I swear it has been sewed onto him. My man is always hot, but by God, when he wears a suit, he just blows me away. Every. Single. Time.

"Ben! You're finally here. You missed all the fun," I tell him regretfully.

"I have not missed a thing. Except maybe you," he tells me as he kisses the tip of my nose. "You look beautiful, Angel, but you must be cold." He shrugs out of his jacket and places it over my shoulders.

"What ya got there?" he asks as he nudges the heart clutched tightly in my hand.

"Oh this is—" I stop talking as the light bulb in my head finally goes on. Of course, a black heart.

Ben sees the recognition in my eyes because he lights up and cups my face. "Angel, what you're holding there so tightly in your beautiful hand is everything that I was, everything that I thought I would always be, and everything you changed with your love. For years, my heart has been black and cold as stone."

I look at him and shake my head softly because I know his heart is anything but cold, and I take my free hand and grip one of his in mine. I nod as he continues.

"I didn't think anyone would be able to love a man like me; broken, angry and cold. But since the very first time I laid eyes on you, I began to feel myself start to thaw. And, as time went on, I realized you had thawed it completely. I no longer prefer the darkness, because you are the light. You brightened my life by being the amazing person you are."

He looks down at his legs and then back into my eyes. "I have not felt whole since I lost my leg. But, Angel, you make me feel as if I have a thousand legs. You make me feel like, leg or no leg, the man I am now, with you, is more whole and complete and a better version of what I was even before my accident. I don't want to wake up another day without you next to me. I don't want to wake up another day without being able to call you mine—officially and legally. So, I am standing here before you, the man that you have fixed, asking you to please consider being mine forever. Give me a chance to brighten your life as you do mine. If you say yes, I promise that I will spend every waking moment of my life trying to make you happy, trying to make you smile, and most definitely loving you in every way you deserve, every single day for the rest of our lives."

Tears are streaming down my face as I watch Ben sink to one knee and present me with a box. "Jillian Baldwin, will you marry me?"

He opens the box to reveal the most beautiful ring I have ever seen, glittering up at me as it sits on a pillow of white satin. The center stone is a large, rose-cut black diamond with a white diamond halo surrounding it. The band itself is lined with little black diamonds and is stunning. It is so perfect for us. I am staring at the ring, sobbing and clutching on to the final clue—my little black stone heart. I'm overwhelmed and speechless and just keep looking from the ring back to Ben.

"Angel, you're kind of leaving me hanging here," he mumbles a little nervously.

I drop to my knees in front of him and cup his face in my free hand.

"There isn't anything I want more in this world than to spend the rest of my life with you. You already own me, Ben. We don't need a ring for that. But, yes, yes! I will marry you! Being your wife, being yours, nothing could make me happier!"

I lean in and our lips crash together, sealing our promise with a kiss. After a few seconds, he pulls back, grins broadly, and then lets out a roar. "She said yes!"

All the doors surrounding the terrace fly open, and the place starts to swarm with our friends and loved ones. I have barely made it back onto my feet when I nearly get tackled by Raeva. She is crying her eyes out. "I can't believe you're getting married," she sobs. "I am so happy. Congratulations."

"Hey, stop hogging the bride-to-be!" Mik jokes as she puts her arms around us both and squeezes tight.

"Show us the ring!" Hannah says excitedly as she joins us.

"Did you guys know about this?" I ask, although, I already know the answer.

"Guilty," Raeva admits.

"Yup, me too," Mikaela says

"I guess that makes me three." Hannah beams.

"Well, girls, thank you for helping Ben make tonight unforgettable," I say with a genuine smile.

We are congratulated by all our family and friends, and I'm completely surprised when I see my mom and dad appear in front of me. Apparently, Ben actually went and asked my dad for my hand in marriage, much to their delight, and he happily said yes. We eat, drink, and celebrate our new engagement. Just a few minutes before midnight, Ben takes me by the arm and leads me to the edge of the roof terrace. His arm snakes around my waist, and he pulls me close as we look upon the New York skyline. The view up here is breathtaking.

He leans down and looks into my eyes. "Were you surprised tonight?"

I smile. "I don't think I have ever been more surprised," I tell him with a smile.

"Good," he says, pleased. "I will continue to try and surprise you for the rest of our lives."

"I will continue to love that," I reply.

Ben kisses the top of my head. "On that note, I have one more surprise for you."

I turn to face him. "You're pregnant?"

Ben chuckles. "Not yet, Angel."

"Oh, that's disappointing," I say with a wink.

"I'm pretty sure we can practice making a baby a little later tonight, though, if you'd like."

Just the promise of seeing him naked has heat pooling between my thighs, and I bite my lip in anticipation. I know Ben has noticed because that cocky smirk on his face says it all. I catch his gaze and marvel for a moment at the beauty of his eyes. If eyes are truly the windows to the soul, then right now, his windows are wide open. He's completely bared himself to me, and I to him; this man who I will spend the rest of my life adoring. Behind us, people start the count down, but we continue to look in each other's eyes.

Ten... nine... eight... seven... six... five... four... three...

"I love you," he whispers as he leans in to take my lips.

...Two... "I love you, too."

...One...

HAPPY NEW YEAR!

ACKNOWLEDGEMENTS

We have a lot to be thankful for, but first and foremost, we are so grateful that we were brought together in this crazy Indie book world and that it created a friendship and a bond between us that not even words can describe. It led us to this amazing collaboration, but goes so way beyond that. We know it's just the beginning of what's to come and we can't wait to share it all with you.

We are both extremely grateful to Stuart Reardon, who not only graces our cover, but also gracefully put up with our long emails and crazy questions and requests. Stuart—you're such a genuinely beautiful person, inside and out, and we thank you for sharing yourself on our cover with your gorgeousness and for helping us to promote our story! #TeamBreakingBenjamin   p.s. Michelle promises to stop asking you to take your shirt off.

Speaking of the cover, we FLOVE Liv Moore from Liv's Shoppe so hard!! You made our cover and teasers look AMAZING!!! Thank you so much!

Of course, the team of #Haymi would never have existed if it was not for our dear friend Helene Cuji from the blog IAMABOOKHOARDER. We thank you not just for bringing us together, but for your continued support throughout our careers. We Flove you!!

There were a couple people that helped us pull all the pages of this book together seamlessly, and we owe them each a huge thank you. Kendra Gaither, thank you for so much for taking the pieces we sent to you and making them whole. I know it wasn't an easy task, but you as always, make it look like it was. We would also like to thank our formatter Leigh Stone for your amazing and fast work!! You always do so amazing, and make our pages look absolutely stunning; thank you!!

We'd both also like to thank our husbands. We spent a lot, and I mean a lot, of time together working on this book, meaning they got even less of us then they already do. But, like the amazing men they are, they gave us the space we needed to grow and flourish and create. For this, we love them and thank them for letting us be exactly who we are. Stephen, there is a lid for every jar, and Haylee is so glad she found hers in you. Doug, through every second, minute, hour and day, Michelle loves you more.

Of course, last but not least, we must thank our readers. We adore you. For not just giving our words a chance, but (a lot of you) for also loving them! For those that love our respective series, this book is for you, we wanted to do something special for you guys and we hope that Breaking Benjamin will also steal your heart!

ABOUT THE AUTHORS

Haylee Thorne

When Haylee Thorne isn't writing her stories, she works proudly as a registered nurse in Kentucky. Haylee loves to read and watch TV (she may or may not be slightly obsessed with anime), and there aren't many movies she has not seen. She's known to enjoy a good glass of champagne, and can eat an unlimited amount of French fries (seriously, it's a problem). When she has some free time (as in time not spend working or writing), Haylee loves spending time with her family and friends.

You can find Haylee on her webpage at
http://hayleethorneauthor.com/
or on Facebook at
https://www.facebook.com/hayleethorneauthor/
or on bookbub at
https://www.bookbub.com/profile/haylee-thorne

Other Books by Haylee

Tomorrow, Book 1 of The Kingsley Series: https://amzn.to/2Lz5EWU

After Tomorrow, Book 2 of The Kingsley Series:
https://amzn.to/2ITCM9V

The Beard: https://amzn.to/2ITRIVu

Reclaiming Tomorrow:
https://www.goodreads.com/book/show/35712006-reclaiming-
tomorrow

Project U.G.L.Y: https://www.goodreads.com/book/show/40037150-
project-u-g-l-y

Michelle Windsor

Michelle Windsor is a wife, mom, and a writer who lives North of Boston with her family. When she isn't hidden away in her office, she's been known to partake in good wine and good food with her family and friends. She's a voracious reader, loves to hike with her German shepherd, Roman, enjoys a good romance movie and may be slightly obsessed with Outlander, okay, and Stuart Reardon too....

You can find Michelle on her webpage at
https://www.authormichellewindsor.com
or on Facebook at
https://www.facebook.com/authormwindsor
or on Bookbub at
https://www.bookbub.com/authors/michelle-windsor

Other Books by Michelle

The Winning Bid, Book 1 of The Auction Series: https://goo.gl/ufsC9B

The Final Bid, Book 2 of The Auction Series: https://goo.gl/oHGWdp

Losing Hope: https://goo.gl/e6LfFo

Love Notes: https://goo.gl/jYfG2L

Tempting Secrets, Book 1 in The Tempted Nights Series:
https://goo.gl/PSggN5